THE LAST RESPONDER

NICHOLAS SAINT

CHAPTER 1

As he stared out the barred window of the M1224 MaxxPro vehicle at yet another barren desert landscape, Nathan Profit was as relaxed as he'd ever been during his time in Afghanistan. It wasn't like there was much to look at; on every side were flat plains of yellowish sand that rolled uninterrupted to the dunes in the distance, and even farther to the hills and mountains that reached upward to the brilliant-blue, cloudless sky. For the most part, one view was very much the same as the next, regardless of which direction you traveled. The only time you could get your specific bearings was in sight of one of the main population centers, like Kabul. He'd been part of countless "sweep & clear" missions during the eighteen months he'd spent in the country, and Operation Brightspot was just another routine reconnaissance assignment like so many that had come before it. As the three-vehicle convoy rocked and rolled along the Afghan road—if you could call it that considering it was more of a dirt and gravel paved track— Nathan contemplated the oncoming end of his second deployment in Afghanistan.

Many youngsters enlisted in the military because it was the only realistic career option for them, a choice that was somewhat forced by a multitude of different factors, and not just because they had a lack of skills, education, were facing jail time, or came from genuine poverty. In a large number of other cases, the decision to join the armed forces was one of expectation, more often than not due to previous generations of the family having been in the military. Nathan wished he had a dollar for every time he heard the phrase, "My old man was a soldier" or "My dad was in the army for X years, and it was just expected I would follow suit." The journey that had led to him sitting in the heavily armored troop carrier was different to most others.

At the age of eighteen, Nathan enrolled in the Louisiana State University School of Medicine and studied there for nearly seven years, completing a four-year Doctor of Medicine degree, and then taking additional courses in Anatomy, Biology, Neurology, and Military Science. His physical prowess was every bit as impressive as his mental ability, and at 6'3 with a muscular build and enviable traits, such as speed, power, and agility, Nathan was also a gifted linebacker for the L.S.U. Tigers. In fact, had he focused as much time, effort, and attention on football as he had on his studies, he would've had a genuine shot at playing professionally. That alluring possibility often proved too tempting for even the most dedicated of scholarly students, and yet that option never once entered his mind.

It was during his time at L.S.U. that Nathan met his eventual wife, Lisa Williamson. She was a year older than him and studying to be a teacher at the L.S.U. School of Education. She had started university in her early twenties, following a pause in her education so she could look after her mother, who suffered from both dementia and other physical issues. When she passed away, Lisa promised she would achieve her goal of becoming a teacher. They were introduced to each other by a mutual friend, and despite being loose acquaintances for around six months, they eventually hit it off at a concert they both attended with a group of friends and became a committed couple who loved each other deeply.

When he finally left education, he had a whole range of professional options available to him in the healthcare world, but Nathan had only one career in mind. As long as he could remember, even as a young child, Nathan was fiercely proud of his country, to the extent that it resulted in a few confrontations during his late teens and early twenties when less patriotic members of society spoke badly of the States. He knew, even before he left high school, that he wanted to go to university, graduate at the top of his class and then join the Marine Corps. Throughout his time in New Orleans, many of his fellow students seemed utterly bemused that he could, and almost certainly would, achieve so much on the academic front, only to go and join the armed forces. To him, it was all about doing your duty for your country. The only question mark was whether he would stay within the military or fulfill his own high expectations before moving on to another career.

When it came to the marines, despite his excellent academic achievements, Nathan wanted to begin at the bottom and work his way up. Starting as a Private First Class in boot-camp, he quickly displayed impressive leadership skills, a tactical awareness that was second to none, an unquestionable ability to positively improvise in even the worst situations, a virtually infallible photographic memory, and a steadfast refusal to quit, no matter what hurdle he had to overcome.

He was eventually stationed at the Marine Corps base in Quantico, Virginia, and about a year after joining, at the age of twenty-six, he married Lisa. Ten months later, she gave birth to their daughter, Charlotte. He progressed to the rank of sergeant in three years and was recently promoted again to staff sergeant, but his military career intentions seemed to confuse his senior officers as much as they had his professors at L.S.U. Numerous members of the top brass had made it clear to him that there was no limit to how far he could progress up the ranks, but despite their best efforts to persuade him to rise higher and faster, Nathan was content where he was. The trio of four-man fire teams that he was in charge of were full of good men he liked, trusted, and respected, and he felt the same for the man directly above him—Lieutenant Lucas Robertson. His position afforded him the opportunity to shape his men into decent soldiers, but he didn't have the burden of serious decision-making.

The previous year, he was sent overseas to Afghanistan for the first time and spent nine months in the country, his tour there split between Bagram air base, Shindand air base and Camp Leatherneck. For some of the marines in his unit, one tour of Afghanistan was enough, but about half of those who served during that first overseas posting stayed together and were eventually sent back around six months later. His platoon began their tour stationed at Shindand and were quickly redeployed to the capital, Kabul, but at the end of their fourth month, they were all shipped out to Forward Operating Base Camp Dwyer, where they spent the next three months battling both Taliban and Al-Qaeda insurgents. It was the most dangerous of the five locations they had been based, but Nathan tried to ignore that fact—at the end of the day, he was there to serve his country and he would go where his country sent him.

The heavily armored vehicle continued to rock back and forth as the convoy thundered toward its intended location. The briefing that morning by Captain Justin Anderson was unusually short, which often meant the operation was nothing more than a formality. According to anonymous intel recently provided to a senior official, hostile insurgents were using a village about sixty miles from the base to covertly store weapons. It was unclear whether the villagers themselves were complicit in hiding the supplies or being forced to do so against their will; as a previously friendly village, he was confident it was the latter. Anderson had finished his short assignment meeting by stating he was well aware that in most instances, by the time they had received and acted upon such information, the weapons and hostile forces were long gone. The mission assigned to the eight men of Alpha and Beta teams, plus Nathan and Lucas as their senior officers, was to make a surprise visit to the largish village and verify whether any stashed arms could be found, and to reassess the friendly/hostile status of the village itself.

Nathan was traveling in the second of the three vehicles with his best friend, Corporal Dwayne Bryant, who was in charge of Alpha team, and two other members of that team. In the lead MaxxPro were Robertson and three privates, while the rear carrier contained the Beta team corporal, Davis McCall, the remaining two privates and an interpreter. Each vehicle also had a driver and an additional marine to man the top-mounted machine gun should the convoy come under fire. As he continued to gaze at the sandy peaks in the distance, the always talkative Dwayne interrupted his train of thought.

"I see you're as calm and relaxed as ever, Nath," stated his best friend from the seat next to him.

"You know me, the mission is the mission, today is no different from any other. If going out on a recce trip like this causes you serious tension and worry, you're probably in the wrong career," chuckled Nathan in response.

He didn't mean to sound cold and heartless, far from it, it was more to do with the fact that he accepted the risks and dangers that came with being a marine… that came with any branch of the armed forces. Nathan knew firsthand from two casualties during his previous tour, that when a soldier allowed his fear to control him, fatal mistakes were never too far behind. He was proud to say that he had no concern about this with any of the present members that made up his three fire teams. Before Dwayne had a chance to indulge in his usual ribbing of his colleague's cool, calm approach, there was a crackle in their in-ear monitors followed by the familiar update from Robertson.

"Okay, people… we're ten minutes out. You know the drill. I want everyone ready to fall out as soon as we get there. We'll sweep the village, house to house, from the northern end down to the south. We were told to expect a welcoming committee of village elders upon arrival, so keep your eyes open but remember… right now, until we know or have cause to think otherwise, the occupants are friendlies."

The three M1224's took a right turn a few minutes later and proceeded along a track that was in even worse condition than the one they had just left. The whole vehicle shook in all directions as it hit one pothole after another. As they got ever closer, Nathan went through his usual routine of double-checking all his equipment—ensuring his helmet chinstrap and flak-jacket were fastened properly, that his ammo clips were all in the right pouches and that he'd securely fastened his grenades, and that all his other equipment was in order. Lastly, he reconfirmed both his black M27 automatic rifle and Beretta M9 sidearm were locked and loaded.

Nathan knew everything was in order, he'd made sure of that before he had climbed into the heavy-duty carrier, but being the judicious soldier he was, it had become routine for him to recheck during the final few minutes of the journey, regardless of whether it was by land transport or helicopter. As the vehicle came to a stop, he put on his black shades that had previously hung by one arm from his flak-jacket, took a swig from his water bottle, and prepared to disembark.

The three vehicles had parked in a defensive semicircle facing the entrance to the village. In the sky above, there was the familiar sound of a Black Hawk helicopter that was providing air support and intel from its hovering vantage point. With their motion stopped, Robertson appeared over the comms again and ordered everyone to exit the vehicles. As the eight men formed into their two teams, Nathan took a moment to gaze over at the target village and size up the situation.

From the outside, it looked like any number of villages he had previously been to. Either side of the main entrance, there was a large sandstone wall that appeared to surround the whole village, apart from the two entrances on either side, or so he assumed. There was a wide, rugged track of flattened sand that ran through the very center of the village and veered off in a curve to the left. On either side of the road were flat-roofed houses and huts made from either sandstone, mud, clay, or timber, and from his vantage point, it looked like there were around forty to forty-five of them within the village.

"Okay, gather round," ordered Robertson from the rear of the vehicles. With Nathan now to his right and the interpreter to his left, the other eight men formed their own semicircle in front of the senior officers. "Just to repeat for the hard of hearing, that'd be you, Nicholson, the intel came with no evidence, so we have no idea if that is true, was true, or just false information by a rival village. Either way, we treat it the same."

As he spoke, a group of five villagers walked through the entrance to the village and made their way toward the marines.

"The previous designation for this village was friendly, so we continue to assume that is the case unless proven otherwise," said Lt. Robertson. "Once we do the customary meet 'n' greet with the elders, we will try to get their approval to do the house-to-house sweep across the village. We'll break into four teams of two… Nathan, you team up with Bryant, I'll go with McCall. I want this done respectfully and with as little pushback from the villagers as possible. Anderson seemed pretty certain all enemy combatants and their stash would be long gone, so let's make sure we don't alienate the village by being heavy-handed over nothing. Understood?"

In unison, the other ten men confirmed with a loud, "Yes, sir!"

The unit of marines met the village elders midway between the M1224's and the village entrance. Through the interpreter, Robertson explained to the villagers about the previously received anonymous information, and that while he was confident that it was false intel, he was still required by his superiors to confirm that assumption. Nathan's attention switched between the conference in front of him and the village itself as he closely inspected what was going on in the background for anything suspicious. The village representatives quickly became upset and were furious to be even remotely accused of aiding or providing assistance to terrorist insurgents. The interpreter explained they were deeply offended about the invasion of privacy and the prospect of having their homes searched, and that they refused to give their permission. That posed a difficulty to Robertson because part of his orders was to not alienate the village. After fifteen tense minutes, following numerous promises about respecting the locals and their homes, the village committee begrudgingly gave their agreement to the search, but they made it clear they wanted the marines to finish their task as quickly as possible and leave.

Following a meeting in the middle of the village where the elders told the rest of its inhabitants what was happening, the marines made their way through the entrance. The unit split into four teams of two, with Nathan and Lucas attached to one on either side, and then they began their house-to-house search. Before entering, the marines asked the occupants to stand outside, which most did without too much fuss, even if their facial expression showed visible irritation as they lined up. Most of the houses had between five and eight family members, usually a husband and a wife, at least a couple of children and one or two older relatives. The buildings themselves often had one large public room and anywhere between two to four other areas.

Everything went exactly as Nathan had expected. Before entering each property, he politely requested permission from the occupants to search their house and asked that they stand outside while they carried out the inspection. Nathan, Dwayne, and Private Kris Romano conducted a thorough search of each abode, but they did it in a way that caused the least mess and were also very careful not to break anything if at all possible;

everyone knew that would quickly cause tensions to rise again rapidly. It took them about ten minutes to search the basic hut-style homes, and once done, they made a huge effort to express their gratitude, via the phrases given to them by the interpreter, before moving on to the next building.

Nathan, Dwayne, and Romano were on their twelfth home when things took a sinister turn. As Nathan searched the side room and Romano the back rooms, Dwayne noticed a creaking sound when he stepped on the edge of a large rug between some mattresses and a table. As far as the marines were aware, the floor of the homes was the solid ground they were actually built on, so the sound of creaking wood immediately raised suspicions. It happened purely by chance when he stepped backward to pick up a child's toy that he'd inadvertently knocked on the floor. Had he stuck to the usual clearway through the room, he would have walked straight past it. Calmly lifting his hand to his radio, he pressed the button and raised the alarm.

"Sarge, LT, we might have a problem. I got a creaking sound coming from the floor in the main room of this house. There must be something wooden under the rug in here. That intel may not be wrong after all, so I suggest you all proceed with caution."

Within seconds, both Nathan and Kris had joined Dwayne in the hut's main public room. Dwayne and Kris moved the table and chairs, then lifted the mattresses into the far corner to create plenty of space. The occupants outside the house began to look increasingly concerned and fidgety, and Nathan had to order Kris to keep a close eye on them while he and Dwayne investigated the interior. Taking a corner of the rug each, the two marines tossed it aside. Underneath was a large, almost perfectly fitted wooden cover that was nearly as big as the huge rug that concealed it. Nathan carefully looked it over for any sign of booby traps, and feeling confident that it was safe, the two of them moved the wooden hatch to the side.

"LT, we've hit pay dirt over here. There is a large, hidden pit under the wooden cover, and there is enough firepower in here to arm a medium-sized militia group. There are loads of AKs, numerous ready-to-go I.E.D.s, several R.P.G.s, boxes of ammunition, grenades… hell, they've even got some of our shit in here," Nathan confirmed to Robertson.

"Okay, calmly and quietly, if possible, escort them down to the vehicles," ordered Robertson. "I want you to get the interpreter to find out why they have all that stuff stashed in their house. The rest of you, continue with your sweep and sound out if you find anything else."

"Copy that," replied Nathan. As the three marines headed for the entrance, the people who lived in the house suddenly started shouting loudly as they ran away from the building toward the other end of the village.

"Lieutenant, we got runners; they've taken off in the direction of the other end of the village. Permission for the three of us to chase them down?" asked Nathan.

"Nathan, hold your position. We're in a pretty vulnerable spot right now, given we're right in the middle of the village. Let's regroup at your location, secure the weapons, and then we'll track them down together."

Nathan ordered the two marines searching the next house up on his side to finish their sweep, and then to drop back and join up with them in his house. On the other side of the road, Robertson instructed his second team to do the same. As Nathan waited for the other pair to appear, he took up a vantage point near the door to see what was going on in the rest of the village. There was a lot of excitable yelling all around, and though he didn't speak the language, it seemed pretty obvious to him that the raised, angry voices must be alarm calls. Seconds later, he was proved right.

From both ends of the village, two groups of around fifteen to twenty armed men began to swarm up the village road. It was conclusive evidence that the houses they had already searched contained both hostile occupants and concealed weapons. Just as everything erupted, the two other marines on that side ducked into Nathan's house.

"LT, we got a shit-storm about to descend upon us. Looks like our discovery has stirred up a real viper's nest. I count around fifteen or so enemy soldiers coming from the north end behind us, and another fifteen to twenty coming up from the south. If we don't make a move fast, we're gonna get caught in a crossfire that'll cut us to shreds. Permission to engage?"

It seemed like a ridiculous question. They were being fired upon by a superior sized force, but Nathan knew he needed his commanding officer's agreement for his men to return fire.

"Go ahead. See if the five of you can get over here. We have a better viewpoint and firing angle around the bend at the group coming from the south," suggested Robertson.

As Nathan confirmed his agreement, bullets began to fly all around the building they were using as cover. They pinged off the mud walls, a puff of dust bouncing up from each impact. Nathan and Dwayne focused their fire on the group coming down the village, while Romano and the other two privates tried to take out the rabble that were making their way up from behind them.

Robertson's voice appeared over the radio again as he called for the M1224s to make their way closer to the village and provide covering fire, so the marines could retreat back to the vehicles. He also asked the Black Hawk to give them additional air support. In a matter of minutes, a full-on firefight had erupted. One of the privates in Nathan's house was shot in the throat by a bullet and collapsed instantly to the floor. As Dwayne and Romano tried to hold off the increasingly confident enemy, Nathan and the other marine did their best to save his life;

unfortunately, their efforts were in vain. Nathan knew they had to move, and he ordered the other private to pick up his colleague's body as they prepared to join the others across the street. In the middle of asking Robertson and his men to provide covering fire, a bullet hit Nathan badly in the left shoulder.

He never saw it coming; there was just this instant puff of red mist that flashed in front of his eyes before he fell to the floor in absolute agony. It was the first time he'd taken a bullet, and despite stories from other soldiers proclaiming that sometimes you didn't even know you were hit… he knew for sure. With Dwayne attending to Nathan's wound, Romano and the other private continued to fire upon both groups of attackers. Suddenly, there was a large explosion from the entrance behind them, and Romano yelled that the insurgents had destroyed one of the M1224s with an R.P.G. As the assailant loaded up a second rocket, Romano took him out with a clean shot to the head. With the others laying down covering fire, the two privates sprinted to the other side of the street. As Dwayne and Nathan were about to do the same, someone lobbed a grenade through the glassless window opening. They managed to make it a few steps across the dirt road by the time it went off; the blast knocked both men off their feet and to the floor. With Robertson's men pinning down the group coming from around the bend, and the M1224 gunners and Black Hawk focusing on the attackers to their rear, three marines raced out to the street to drag Nathan and Dwayne into the building. Dwayne was initially quite stunned before quickly coming round, but Nathan had been knocked unconscious and also hit by two pieces of shrapnel in his side.

Over the next ten minutes, the intense machine gun fire and even a couple of close-call R.P.G. rockets kept the marines totally pinned down. During that time, the insurgents took out two marines; they shot P.F.C. Nicholson in the neck, killing him almost instantly, and McCall's life ended when a bullet obliterated his face. It placed Robertson in an unenviable position. There was a code within the marines that you never left anyone behind, but with Nathan unresponsive and out of action, plus Dwayne also limited as he carried his friend, there simply wasn't enough manpower to carry their dead comrades from the scene. Robertson made the decision to leave their bodies behind. With two pairs alternating cover fire and the lieutenant helping Dwayne carry Nathan, the seven marines fought their way from the middle of the village to the entrance, where the remaining two M1224s were parked. They had managed to kill the group of insurgents who attacked the marines from the rear, and could now focus their destructive firepower straight down the main village track at the ever-growing number of hostiles coming from the other end.

With the assistance of the two M1224 guns, the marines were able to move past the final few houses quickly and had positioned themselves behind the relative safety of the thick wall surrounding the village. Nathan had begun to regain consciousness, but he still needed Dwayne and another marine to help carry him due to his injuries. The vehicles had moved as close as possible without losing their advantageous firing position, but there was still a reasonable amount of open space for the seven marines to cover before they reached the safety of their armored MaxxPro carriers. The two privates went first, so they could also fire upon their assailants in the village, then Robertson and one of the remaining P.F.C.s followed next. With the mounted machine guns and four marines all unloading their ammunition upon the enemy soldiers down the street, the final three broke cover. About halfway to safety, a bullet struck Dwayne in the back of the leg, and the three of them fell to the floor. Another round quickly hit Nathan, this time in the right leg, and he screamed out in pain, the intensity of the injury fully shaking him awake. One marine was able to drag Dwayne to safety, but just as he was about to return for Nathan, an R.P.G. rocket hit the wall, throwing debris and dust in all directions.

The smoke provided temporary cover for the enemy forces to close in on the two vehicles. With bullet after bullet pinging off the armored carriers and the rest of the marines in grave danger, Robertson looked over at the bleeding, completely still body of Nathan Profit. He also observed that the number of opposition fighters continued to increase, despite multiple casualties, and it was obvious to Robertson that weapons were not the only thing hidden within the village and its immediate surroundings. The lieutenant quickly contemplated whether someone could safely reach Nathan to confirm if he was alive or not, but even with additional fire from the Black Hawk and M1224 guns, he wasn't sure anyone could get to him without genuinely risking their own life. When a pair of R.P.G. rockets narrowly missed the two M1224s, Robertson had to make the decision to retreat. Under protest from Dwayne, the remaining marines quickly climbed into the vehicles and with their gunners still unloading, they reversed away from the village. In the dust and sand that was kicked up by their tires as they made a rapid retreat, no one observed Nathan when he lifted one of his arms, a desperate attempt from a severely injured man to signal that he was still alive. The last he saw of his fellow marines was the two sand-colored carriers speeding off down the road to safety.

With the American soldiers beaten back, the enemy fighters whooped and hollered with joy as they fired their weapons in the air to celebrate their victory. They dragged the three dead marines into the street, stripped them of all their weapons and uniforms, and then paraded them around the village. A group of six men walked toward Nathan with the intention of doing the same to him, but when they rolled him over, the angry mob quickly realized he was still alive… although it wouldn't be long before Nathan Profit wished that he had shared the same fate as his three fallen comrades.

CHAPTER 2

Having removed his weapons, the six men dragged the badly injured marine by the ankles back into the village and dumped him in the center of the road. Nathan was still too dazed to fully absorb the situation that was unfolding, but it was impossible for him to ignore all the shouting and the shadows of multiple people who blocked out the sun as they jumped around his body. His mind bounced from images of the wife and child he loved dearly to regretful acceptance that his life was at an end. He wasn't scared to die and knew that this was a distinct possibility every time he left the safety of the bases in Afghanistan, and yet the reality proved very different to what he'd expected. They talk about someone's life flashing before their eyes at the end, but Nathan wasn't seeing events from his past, more thinking about the things he wouldn't now do, such as seeing his daughter grow up and become a woman, getting the chance to select a new career when his time was over in the marines—something he'd increasingly thought about—to grow old himself, disgracefully probably, with his life-loving wife. He would now have to be content with imagining it all during the last few minutes of his life.

Nathan was so lost in his thoughts that he didn't notice when the yelling and manic behavior of those crowding around him began to wind down. To his left, the villagers parted and four men walked toward him. He squinted as he looked up, and while he couldn't see clearly, he could tell that two of the quartet were village elders from the committee that greeted his unit when they arrived. The appearance of the other two men was somewhat different to that of everyone else in the village. Their clothing was similar to his own combat uniform, complete with shades and a holstered side-arm. The way they spoke to the two senior villagers was calm yet authoritative, but in his less coherent state and with only a basic understanding of the language, it was impossible for Nathan to work out what was being said.

After a few minutes of conversation, the large mob of excitable villagers began to disburse. A couple of men brought out a stretcher from one of the houses, and they lifted Nathan onto it and carried him to a hut at the far end of the village. The unexpected turn of events left him surprised and concerned in equal measure. Several minutes later, two women and a man, the latter also dressed in military fatigues, entered the building. They began to treat Nathan's injuries, and as a medically trained person himself, he could tell that the man giving instructions to the other two ladies clearly knew what he was doing. They removed his uniform, and first attended to the nasty bullet wound in his left shoulder, cleaning it, stitching it up and finally covering it. The two women treating him repeated the same process for the injuries to his right leg and his side where he was hit by shrapnel. When the man was completely satisfied that they had adequately dealt with any physical trauma, he checked on Nathan's potential concussion from the blast and his general condition. Before they left the room, the man gave Nathan three different injections. One was almost certainly an antibiotic, maybe two, and when he felt drowsy within a few minutes, he guessed the third was probably a light form of sedative. As he drifted away from consciousness, Nathan felt someone clamp a large shackle around his left ankle. His final thoughts were those of suspicion about his captors' intentions. They clearly didn't want Nathan dead, but they certainly didn't want him going anywhere, either. The last thing he heard was the voices of three Afghan men as they walked away from the hut.

Within what he assumed were a few days, the insurgents moved Nathan from the village where they ambushed his unit to another similarly looking enclave; he had no idea how far away or where it was located. Nathan quickly lost track of time, partly because he wasn't always conscious, be it sleeping or drug induced, but also because the days simply rolled into one. They had taken his watch from him, and this denied him the last vestige of knowledge when it came to the day and date, although the position of the sun that streamed through the hut's entrance at least gave him some idea of what hour it was. He spent the majority of the time in the same building, shackled by a chain to a large concrete stone; the only freedom he was allowed from his restraints was when he went to the restroom or walked around outside, at first by makeshift crutches, as a form of physical therapy. He did his best to familiarize himself with his surroundings each time he was allowed outside. It was obviously another village, and yet it looked pretty much the same, as did the landmarks in the distance. His observations provided him with no intel or information whatsoever.

The people holding him captive continued to treat his injuries carefully and properly, and the closer he got to full health, the more he became uneasy about their overall intentions. By his best guess, around four to five weeks had passed by the time they finally revealed those aims. One afternoon, the same man who'd stood over him in military dress after he'd been dragged into the village, or at least as best as he could tell from his foggy memories, came into the hut, and sat on a chair facing his bed.

"Good morning, Mr. Profit. My name is Khalid Abdul Nasser Hasan, and I am the senior commander of the resistance forces in this area. We were aware of your impending arrival from sources within your own base, and were content to allow you to conduct your illegal search and move on. Unfortunately for you, your accidental discovery of our supplies forced my men and I to react. Much glory has been heaped on those freedom fighters that killed your infidel compatriots. Your military made a feeble attempt to clear the village a week later, but we had long since moved on."

The man spoke in a very relaxed manner and his English was excellent, something that gave Nathan the idea that he must have been educated abroad.

"Why have you kept me prisoner here?" asked Nathan. "I am genuinely grateful for you treating my wounds, but I demand, under the Geneva Convention, that you release me."

"There it is… the American and Western arrogance that you demand the rest of the world conducts itself by your rules," said Khalid, his tone now containing a noticeable sneer. "We saved your life so that you may provide us with the knowledge and information we desire to aid us in our holy mission to rid our country of your presence and interference. Starting tomorrow, you will tell us everything that we ask, or the pain you suffered from your wounds will be nothing to what is inflicted upon you," Khalid warned.

"If you think a U.S. marine will actively collude with enemy forces, then you're going to be considerably disappointed. I'd rather die than tell you anything of importance," replied Nathan with conviction.

"By the time we're finished with you, I guarantee you'll be begging for us to end your suffering."

Khalid walked swiftly from the hut, the intention obviously being to allow his words to fester in Nathan's mind for the rest of the day. He struggled to sleep that night, and despite his confidence in his own strength and resolve, it was impossible to ignore that every man had a breaking point. Over and over again, he began to repeat false information so that it became automatic. It was his hope that if he reached the point where he couldn't take it any longer, then at least his false intel would be consistent.

He was given his usual breakfast the next morning and though he wasn't hungry, he forced himself to eat it so he wouldn't show any sign of apprehension or worry. An hour later, two armed men came into the hut, unshackled him, and forcefully took him from that house to another. It was visually similar to the previous building they'd kept him in, but the contents of this had nothing to do with recovering from his injuries. There was a stout metal chair in the center of the room, and the guards stripped him naked and bundled Nathan into it, his wrists and ankles tied with thick rope to either the arms or the legs. To his left was a wooden table with various fear-inducing implements, and in front of him was a smaller table with a more comfortable looking chair behind it. The two guards walked out the door and left Nathan alone for several minutes. They eventually returned and stood behind his chair, swiftly followed by Khalid and the man who'd overseen his recovery.

"Good afternoon, Mr. Profit, I take it your time alone in this room has left you acutely aware of your predicament. I hope you will see reason, and we can avoid the worst of the unpleasantness that awaits you. Now, let's begin with something simple. What is your name?" asked the Afghan commander.

"Nathan Douglas Profit... Staff Sergeant, United States Marine Corps... Identification Number 100500809..."

"There, you see, how hard was that?" mocked Khalid. "So, how many men in your unit, your platoon, and your company?"

"Nathan Douglas Profit... Staff Sergeant, United States Marine Corps... Identification Number 100500809..." repeated Nathan.

"Ah, yes, the famous three important details on repeat. Let's try again, then I am afraid that things will have to start getting ugly. How many men in your unit, your platoon, and your company?" asked Khalid again.

"Nathan Douglas Profit… Staff Sergeant, United States Marine Corps… Identification Number 100500809…"

"Standing to my right is Dr. Taimur Azfaar Samandy. As you already know, he is a fine doctor, but he is also very adept at causing pain and injury without fatally wounding someone, unless he needs to. You are about to experience Dr. Samandy's other most interesting aspects," stated Khalid proudly.

Samandy picked up a portable blow-torch and held it over the end of a large knife for a couple of minutes, then without warning, he placed the burning hot blade on Nathan's stomach. He screamed out in pain and sweat immediately started to pour from his forehead.

"I ask you again," began Khalid.

The session lasted nearly three hours. The insurgents' senior officer wanted to know troop numbers, the amount of equipment available within Camp Dwyer and its capabilities, deployment plans, security procedures and any other useful information that Nathan might know. Despite several burns, a burning blade driven straight through the palm of his hand and several vicious blows to the face from a large, muscular soldier —who was "invited to join the party"—Nathan refused to give any information.

"Your friends left you for dead, Nathan. They saw you lying there, still alive, and they left you behind. Why do you protect the people who failed to protect you?" questioned Khalid.

He was left to think on that question for a few minutes, then taken back to his usual hut and shackled to the block again. Absorbing the physical torture had taken a lot out of Nathan, and he soon passed out. The guards threw a bucket of water over him when they delivered his evening meal, and again not wishing to show any sign of weakness, he forced himself to eat it.

For weeks on end, he was subjected to the same treatment every other day, sometimes even daily. He was given food in the morning, tortured during the afternoon, and then returned to his room for the rest of the day. The majority of the torture was physically related, ranging from Samandy using scalding hot items to burn Nathan's skin, through pulling his fingers out of joint one by one before breaking at least three on each hand, to beatings with fists, bats, canes, and bars. On one occasion, they even dislocated his shoulder just to put it back in its socket again. Other recognized attempts at extracting the required information included water-boarding, cuts and slices, electric shocks to various parts of his body, and even drugs that made his nerves feel like they were on fire. At times, Nathan gave them a few snippets of information that he knew were either meaningless or falsely concocted in his mind. He never gave up hope that he would eventually be rescued if he could just hold out long enough.

When they were not physically abusing him. Khalid waged a war on his mental state. In the early days, when his mind was still clear and functioning, he was well aware of the brainwashing tactics that were being used, but as the days passed, he began to struggle to fight back the never-ending mind games that were being inflicted upon him. After a while, he was tied up, blindfolded, and taken to another location; Nathan's best guess was that it took five to six hours to reach the new destination. He was thrown in what appeared to be a proper cell with metal bars and concrete walls, one of several in the room where he was imprisoned. He was still given food and water, and two days later, the routine of questioning and torture resumed once again. Khalid was still in charge of the session, but this time there were two "doctors" who were responsible for his physical abuse—Samandy and Dr. Bahnam Jaah Tabish Qasim, a man who clearly relished his role.

Over the next six months, Nathan's treatment got steadily worse. They resorted to breaking other bones (forearm) or damaging ligaments (knee), and when they had badly hurt him, they left him alone to heal a little before they started all over again. The repeated beatings left his face regularly swollen, and he often couldn't see out of both eyes. A couple of times he was strung up by his wrists and punched so hard and so often that his ribs cracked. Sometimes, they refused to give him food or water, telling him he'd be left to rot and die in the cell, and they would leave him guessing for a day or two, occasionally longer when it came to food. Sleep deprivation became another unrelenting tool of abuse; during one eight-day stretch, he wasn't allowed to sleep for more than sixty minutes. Everything they did took him just the right side of fatal or irreversible. Eventually, the lies and made-up replies began to turn into real information. He tried his hardest to limit what he said, but there were days when he couldn't even remember what had happened, the various injuries his only reminder of what had occurred.

He was moved at least two more times during his incarceration, and each new location was much the same. A solid building in a decently built enclave, but somewhere that appeared off the beaten track. There were three instances when he was aware he wasn't the only captive that was being tortured, the screams of pain coming through the constantly locked door providing ample evidence that others were suffering at the hands of Khalid and his accomplices. One of the other prisoners must have been a high-value target because a covert U.S. Special Forces team mounted a rescue attempt to free that one man. Nathan's cell in that particular building had a barred open window, and he screamed with all his might at the soldiers guarding the helicopter that landed in the courtyard; one soldier even looked directly at him, but assuming it was some form of trick, he ignored the pleas for help. The rescue team killed several insurgent fighters during the raid, although Khalid and his two medical enthusiasts survived. That was the moment Nathan Profit's willpower finally broke.

Over a year had passed since he was captured in the remote village, and he had endured unimaginable treatment during that time. Throughout it all, he had held out hope that one day, be it intentionally or by accident, he would be rescued by the American or N.A.T.O. forces. To be so close to that and left behind was more than he could stomach. He felt abandoned, that the world had forgotten all about him. It didn't really register with him any longer that he would be considered dead by the American military—a fellow brother-in-arms had looked right into his eyes and left him behind. The insurgents who survived the assault quickly moved again the next day and when the mistreatment resumed, Nathan slowly began to provide ever more classified information. In part, he no longer saw why he should protect those who left him behind, but the tiny remnant of the man he used to be also assumed his information was probably long out of date anyway.

As more weeks passed and his information dried up, the horrendous treatment slowly changed from being used as a way to gather intel to pure enjoyment for those carrying it out. He could no longer provide them with anything of use, and yet Khalid continued to drag him in for sessions. What was once done for a specific reason quickly became more about brainwashing him and the entertainment of the doctors than anything specifically useful. He no longer cared what happened to him. Mentally, emotionally, and physically, he could endure no more. The broken, lifeless soul in front of Khalid no longer served any purpose, and he eventually unveiled the final act of his twisted, fifteen-month exercise.

"Nathan, you have provided us with endless amusement and fun, a chance to try out things on a human being we never thought could be endured, but our time together is almost at an end. The information you eventually gave up will be put to good use... be sure that many of your compatriots will perish thanks to your assistance. Now, you can serve our cause one more time. It is my intention to provide your superiors with proof you are still alive, then in front of the whole world, we will execute you," confirmed Khalid.

He was thrown back in his cell, and except for the bare minimum of food and water that was chucked in, they left Nathan to think about his fate. Having seen what had happened during previous online executions by similar groups, he knew the likely method would involve a savage beheading. He tried to avoid looking scared and anxious in the hope they wouldn't drag it out, but now he just wanted it to end.

A week later, he was dragged half-conscious from his cell and made to kneel in front of a video camera. Five masked men walked into shot and surrounded him, then the one in the center read a lengthy speech in a foreign language; from the voice, Nathan knew it was Khalid. He twice placed a large, extremely sharp blade to Nathan's throat, giving the genuine impression his head was about to be hacked off, only to suddenly take it away again. With the ringing of laughter in his ears, the masked figures returned Nathan's almost limp body to his cell. Enjoying the psychological torture, Khalid and his men repeated the same process two days later, and two more mock executions—a firing squad and a hanging—were both started before they were also halted to the great amusement of those taking part.

Two days after his walk to the unused noose, Nathan and the insurgents moved location yet again, this time returning to a far more rural setting and a village that was slightly smaller than the one where his ordeal started. He was kept in a windowless hut with two guards permanently standing outside. One evening, another male joined him in the building. The American man introduced himself as Erik Whelan and explained that he was a Middle East arms dealer. He was wanted by another faction in Afghanistan and was being hidden overnight by Khalid and his followers. Nathan was barely able to speak as he had hardly uttered a word in weeks. Erik admitted he was no saint, but he was appalled when he found out some of what Nathan had been through.

"My business in Afghanistan and my deals with Khalid's group are almost over. I promise, if there is any way I can manage it, I will do everything I can to get you out of here," he whispered quietly.

Nathan didn't really care if he was telling the truth or not because his hopes of freedom died many months earlier. During the night, two different groups of men came to the village looking for the arms dealer. With three large deals to be completed in the coming weeks, Khalid denied all knowledge of Erik. He left the next day, but reiterated his commitment to setting Nathan free just before the insurgents came to get him.

Khalid seemed to have tired of abusing the American marine and the frequency of his torture began to decrease rapidly; instead, his wounds went untreated, and he was left to rot in the dark hut. They did at least give him food and water, and this provided evidence to Nathan that they still wanted him for something… most probably the live execution that would be broadcast over the web to ramp up fear around the world.

Erik came to the village twice over the next couple of weeks, and both times took refuge in the same hut in case those who wanted him came looking. He arrived each time in a truck loaded with weapons that Khalid's men hid overnight. Before he left the second time, he told Nathan to be ready to go when he next heard the arrival of a similar vehicle. Another week passed and one afternoon, as he was slumped half-conscious against the wall, he heard the engine of a large truck. Nathan refused to allow himself to believe a single word about any rescue, and he was sure that Erik was all talk; after all, why would he risk his own life for Nathan? The two insurgents no longer guarded the hut because Khalid felt it was a waste of manpower, so they had resumed shackling Nathan to a large concrete block. An hour or two passed and there was no sign of Erik.

"Just as I thought," mumbled Nathan to himself.

Minutes later, the door slowly opened, and an unknown man quietly entered the hut. He knelt down in front of Nathan and began picking the lock to his ankle restraint.

"Afternoon, mucker. Me name's Ian and I work with Erik," said the man in a thick Australian accent. "While he's busy with Khalid and his mates finishing the deal, he told me to come and sneak you to the truck. We ain't stoppin' overnight, we're out of here as soon as his deal's done."

Nathan assumed it was another sick joke by Khalid, but the involvement of a new face gave him just enough hope to accept the offer of help. Once he was freed from the chain, Ian helped Nathan up. The Aussie had a quick look outside and waited for an opportune moment to carry the broken American to the truck. With the coast clear, he put Nathan's right arm around his neck and the two of them left the hut. The vehicle was only ten or twelve steps away, Erik intentionally "forgetting" he should have parked on the other side. Ian had just a minute or two to push Nathan up into the truck, and he managed it with seconds to spare. Acting as if nothing was amiss, he mooched around the vehicle until Erik returned.

"Did you get him?" Nathan heard him ask.

"The package is aboard. I got no idea why we're risking our lives for this, but I owed you big time. After this, mate, we's even," replied Ian

"I'd like to think if we were in his state, if we'd been through even half of what he has, that someone would take pity and do the right thing for us. Now, let's motor on out of here. We'll take the usual route to start, then change course to throw 'em off in case they realize he's gone in the next few hours. If we're lucky, they'll decide not to feed him today."

The two cab doors opened and slammed shut, then the truck rumbled into life. Nathan felt the motion as it moved away, and he knew he was on the cusp of freedom. There was still some doubt within him whether it was all real, but as the seconds turned to minutes, as ten minutes became thirty, he knew that the rescue was genuine and that he was actually free. His journey in the truck continued on through the night and into the next day. After the first pit-stop to refuel using the cans in the back, Erik gave Nathan a blanket and pillow, plus some food and water.

"You rest in the back. We've taken a totally different route to the one they will expect. They'll never find us now, I promise you… well, not unless they have access to some aircraft that I don't know about," Erik assured him.

Nathan broke down in tears as he repeatedly thanked Erik and Ian for what they had done. They drove north for nearly two days and finally stopped at a safe house that only Erik knew about. He'd already prepared for Nathan's arrival and had stocked up on medical supplies to treat his various wounds. He even arranged for an English doctor he trusted implicitly to make regular visits to deal with the worst of the abuse. It took Nathan's body nearly three weeks before it began to show any real improvement, but Erik knew the mental scars would last for years, if not for the rest of his life. With regular visits from the doctor, proper food and drink, plenty of rest and even a few trips to a private clinic through Erik's trusted network of contacts, Nathan was on the mend.

As the right time approached, Erik explained to Nathan that he was wanted by the American authorities, among many others, so he couldn't just drop him off at a N.A.T.O. base. When Nathan was ready, he was moved to an abandoned house in Kabul, and Erik passed an anonymous tip to a senior officer in the American military. Less than twenty-four hours later, a squad of American marines stormed the building to find

Nathan Profit—a soldier everyone thought was dead—alive and waiting to be rescued.

The badly traumatized marine was utterly overwhelmed with relief during the first few days and struggled to speak to anyone about his ordeal. He was moved to a fully functioning hospital, where medics and surgeons spent weeks treating some of the more severe injuries. As he recovered, he was taken through the debriefing process, but it still proved too much for him. Those who regularly dealt with the victims of extreme torture suggested it might help for him to be flown home; the top brass agreed. Nearly two years after he was first captured, Nathan boarded the plane that would fly him back to the United States.

CHAPTER 3

Due to Nathan's extreme experience, senior officials felt it would be beneficial to fly him home via a private plane. Word had already spread in the press that a marine who was previously confirmed as "killed in action" two years earlier had since been found alive, and he would have walked straight into the public eye had he taken a commercial flight. There were more regular military flights, but after everything he'd been through, senior officials deemed the relative calm and obscurity of a private jet to be the best option.

He took a long look around Bagram air base from the top of the stairs, a last glance at a country he had no intention of ever returning to, and yet he knew the large part of him that died somewhere in the Afghan wilderness would never leave. Even though he was now in absolute safety, Nathan struggled to relax. The plane had only been in the air an hour when a stewardess dropped a silver tray and Nathan almost jumped out of his seat.

"It is going to take time," he told himself under his breath.

His terrorist captors had taken everything way from Nathan during his incarceration, and now he had a deep appreciation of even the smallest thing, like a glass of fresh water whenever he wanted it or something to eat as soon as he asked. The old adage that you never really know what you've got until you lose it couldn't have been truer. Ever since he'd first met Erik, Nathan had found it took real, serious effort to talk to people because he had become so used to his isolation. Even now, many weeks later, a simple conversation with the staff on the plane was exhausting. As he settled back in his chair, he tried to listen to music, something he hadn't done in years, but nothing seemed to give him the pleasure he expected when he put the headphones on. Two of his favorite bands had released new albums, something that previously would have delighted him and caused real excitement; instead, he got a track into both and just turned them off. He was well aware that his totally distracted mind was part of the reason behind his struggle to enjoy music… to enjoy anything.

Nathan knew that there were many more weeks of information debriefing ahead, with everyone from his old commanding officer to the resident shrink, and that was before you included the countless medical appointments he would go through with various doctors and specialists. Eventually, now the news of his dramatic rescue had made headlines around the globe, he would also have to speak to the press; how would he cope talking to complete strangers who would print every word he said? Khalid and his followers now knew he'd been rescued— might they make an attempt on his life once he was back home? He still had to face the men who left him behind, a decision he was already increasingly angry about. If it had been one of the others, Nathan knew he would have found a way to ensure whether they were actually dead or not, and even if they did leave to save themselves, someone should have immediately green-lit a mission to clear the village and reclaim the bodies of the fallen marines. The fallen marines… that was the very first time he'd even thought about the three men who died that day. Were their bodies ever recovered?

That was enough to preoccupy anyone's mind, but there was one consideration that stood above everything else—his wife and daughter. Nathan had repeatedly spoken about Lisa and Charlotte from the moment he was rescued, and asked those in charge numerous times about when he would be allowed to speak to them? Throughout his recovery period in Afghanistan, the same answer was always given—that it had been a massive shock for Lisa to find out Nathan was still alive and that in the immediate aftermath, she needed time to come to terms with the unexpected news. With every month that passed during his ordeal, he accepted there was an ever greater chance that she would have moved on with her life; the realist in him knew the ongoing lack of contact proved his worst fears. It was another aspect that added more fuel to his anger over what had happened. He tried to hide it from the shrinks, pretending he understood that things may well have changed, but the rage that began just a day or two after he was rescued grew each and every day. No matter what decisions Lisa had made, Charlotte was still his daughter and there was no way he had any intention of allowing her to be completely taken away from him.

He had plenty of time to think about what he would say to Charlotte and Lisa on his journey home. The luxury of a private jet meant the flight time was substantially less than a similar distance for someone using commercial airlines. The private plane left Bagram, and it took around six and a half hours for it to fly 5,200 km northwest to Ramstein air base in Germany. The stopover was as much about giving Nathan a break from being confined to the aircraft as it was about refueling. The base commander had granted special permission for him to leave the plane and spend some time on the tarmac. He was given the opportunity of extending the break, so he could visit the Kaiserslautern Military Community Center with its sports lounge, bakery and food courts, but Nathan was content just to enjoy the fresh air sitting near the hangar and the parked jet.

The second leg of his journey was the 6,500 km from Ramstein to Joint Base Andrews in America, a flight that would take around eight hours. As the kilometers reduced and the arrival time got ever nearer, he became increasingly apprehensive. They had already told Nathan that familiar people would be there to greet him, but knowing it wouldn't be Lisa or Charlotte, he wondered who it might be. It couldn't be his parents because they had both passed away not long after Charlotte was born. His father had a fatal heart attack and his mother died in her sleep about eight months later; the official cause was a respiratory disease, although Nathan always maintained it was from a broken heart at the loss of her husband. Based on the fact he was landing at a high security military base, he could only conclude it must be one or two of his old unit. Just what could he say to the men that he considered had left him to die? By the time he was informed that they would be landing in an hour, Nathan had already answered that question, and it was the same answer that he came to with the medical staff in Afghanistan—he would say exactly what they expected him to say!

Before he knew it, the majority of those sixty minutes had passed, and the jet made its descent into Joint Base Andrews. As he felt the wheels skid on the tarmac when they touched down, Nathan closed his eyes and let out a deep breath. He was finally home, although it didn't feel the way he expected when he was locked away in his cells and huts. Nathan had imagined that the moment he reached home-soil would be one to savor, one of those moments in life that are extra special. Prior to giving up all hope, Nathan had visualized it in his head over and over again, seeing himself jump out of his seat at the exact moment the plane juddered, and the rubber wheels screeched. He'd always thought he'd be hugging people around him, originally assuming it would be a commercial flight or military transport, and whooping for joy. He saw himself almost shaking with excitement to see his wife and daughter, wishing away every moment between landing and first setting eyes on them.

Nathan had always dismissed the notion when he heard someone say that romantic, world-stands-still moments when lovers initially meet were pieces of pure fiction that never happened in the real world; they did, and he knew that because he had experienced it. Like a projection playing in the back of his mind, one of the memories Nathan had clung to before he abandoned all hope was his arrival home after his first tour. His unit had landed at the same base the previous year, and thanks to their involvement in a very successful tour, the military had allowed their families onto the tarmac to greet their loved ones as they disembarked. He vividly remembered how he walked through the plane's hatch and momentarily paused at the top of the portable stairs. He scanned the crowd and took just seconds to spot Lisa and Charlotte. Immediately, he flashed his smile at them, then descended slowly down the stairs. As he stepped onto the tarmac and walked in their direction, the world did slow down. He saw her long, brown hair waft and pretty teal skirt flutter in the light breeze. Her grin was as wide as the Grand Canyon when she leaned down and pointed him out to Charlotte. He remembered how he wrapped his arms around her, and they kissed for what seemed like an eternity before the pair of them stopped and stared into each other's eyes. Another phrase he'd often heard was his fellow marines telling him they wished they had a "love like that" whenever they'd seen Nathan and Lisa together.

There would be no fairy-tale styled romantic reunion when he returned this time. He'd yet to even speak to Lisa and was still none the wiser as to her situation. The man he used to be might have hoped that maybe there was an unexpected surprise waiting for him when he stepped from the plane, but the quacks had made it absolutely clear before he left that Lisa and Charlotte would not be there. He remained almost motionless in his seat as the plane came to a stop, having completed its landing. The pilot came over the intercom and offered his congratulations that Nathan was home, while the two stewardesses both clapped and grinned at him. Nathan offered his appreciation to all of them for bringing him home, but inside it felt more like a funeral than a celebration. He was a different man to the one that left, even to the one that fought so hard during the early months of his incarceration, and his entire existence back home would be as alien as the lives of those in the country he just left.

The plane slowly taxied around for a few minutes until it came to a dead stop. The pilots appeared from the cockpit and the crew of the plane formed a line, almost like a guard of honor, that led to the door. He lifted himself out of the comfy chair and slowly, step by step, made his way to the exit. Nathan had experienced all sorts of apprehension and anxiety during his time as a prisoner, but the sensations swirling around inside were the strongest he'd ever felt. It was like the polar opposite of his previous return; that time, he couldn't wait to get off the plane and see his family… on this occasion, he wouldn't have minded if time slowed right down and he didn't have to face the welcoming committee for another few hours. Unfortunately, this was real life and not science-fiction, and now, like a log dragged down the rapids of America's famous rivers, Nathan was powerless to swim against the tide.

He stepped out into the cool East Coast climate; it was sunny, but there was a crispness to the air that he hadn't experienced in so long. He gazed around the base before turning his attention to the group that were gathered about 200 yards from the bottom of the stairs. The base had initially wanted to make it quite an occasion, there was even talk of a marching band, but Nathan pleaded with his doctors to ensure his arrival was a low-key affair. Instead of countless dignitaries, the majority of whom he'd probably never even met, there was a small group comprising ten people. His sight was still recovering from long periods in the dark and all the beatings, but he could tell the majority of them were senior officers and probably medical staff; however, there were two faces he did recognize.

Standing at the front were the familiar figures of Lt. Robertson and Dwayne. Had he really given it some thought, it should have been obvious that the two of them would be there to welcome him home, assuming nothing had happened to them during the two years he was locked away. You couldn't miss Robertson, who was 6'6 and built like the proverbial outhouse. The dark-skinned lieutenant would normally flash his trademark wicked smile when he first saw you, and while it was obvious he was pleased to see Nathan, his face looked more shocked than happy. Dwayne was another man who wasn't exactly average sized. His muscular 6'4 frame often towered above those around him, except when he was with Robertson. The fact they were dressed in military uniform told Nathan they were both still enlisted, and despite his sight difficulties, he even spotted some sergeant's stripes on Dwayne's uniform.

Nathan stopped momentarily when both feet were standing on the tarmac and he tried to savor the moment, but no matter how hard he forced it, the pleasure of his homecoming just wasn't there. He still had something of a limp from all the injuries his body had suffered, although the medics had told him he would make a full recovery in time if he worked hard. He walked over to his comrades, stood in front of them and forced a smile across his face.

"Fuck me, Nath, we all thought you were dead," confessed Dwayne. "I never thought in a million years I'd ever see you again, my friend."

He wasn't usually one for outpourings of emotion, but this was obviously a unique situation. He leaned forward and gave Nathan a big hug, patting him on the back as he did.

"Man, I can't even come up with the words to tell you how happy I am to see you, Nath. When they called me up and told me that a Special Ops team had found you in an abandoned building in Kabul, I was sure there had to be a mistake. I am so sorry, Nathan; if we'd known you were still alive on the ground, we would never have left you behind. No words can make up for that, but I hope you'll be able to forgive all of us one day," said his old friend.

Dwayne had genuinely cried tears of happiness when he received the initial call that Nathan was still alive, and they didn't need to ask him to be there for his friend's arrival because he volunteered before they had finalized the initial plans. During his briefing, he was told about some of the things that Nathan had been through and warned about his shocking physical state. Dwayne thought he was ready for that, but nothing could prepare him for the reality that stood in front of him that afternoon. Nathan still had visible scars in rather prominent places, his eyes were set back in their sockets and surrounded by black rings, and he'd lost a substantial amount of his weight and muscular physique. He was horrified to see the after-effects of the brutality that Nathan had endured. In addition, Dwayne had to temper his obvious relief about his friend's unexpected survival with the extreme guilt that surfaced less than an hour after that call. Dwayne knew he'd vehemently urged the lieutenant to confirm Nathan's status, and the whole unit was at risk if they tried, but he'd consoled himself with the knowledge that his friend was dead; they had left his body behind, not the man.

"Hey, D, it's good to see you, buddy. I'm sorry you have to see me like this, but I am glad you're here to meet me. It means a lot," replied Nathan.

Did he mean that? He honestly didn't know. It was good to see his old friend, but the words also felt forced...

"Staff Sergeant Profit, welcome home," said Robertson with his hand outstretched. "Like Sergeant Bryant, I will never be able to apologize enough for taking the decision to leave. I assure you, I did not take the decision lightly, and I would have made a different call had I known for sure you were still alive. It really is good to see you, Nathan. Your country owes you more than it can ever repay. For now, let's get you settled on the base, so you can get some rest after your flight."

Nathan had become accustomed to falseness and words that were spoken because they were expected and not sincere, and there was something about Robertson's greeting that didn't sit right. It was almost as if he was projecting the same "said because I should" facade that Nathan had put on.

"Thank you, sir. It is good to be home. There are a number…" began Nathan.

"I know, Nathan, there are lots of things you want to attend to and deal with. We will get to that, I promise you. Right now, the medical staff and top brass have suggested you spend a few days getting used to being back home, and then we can start helping you put your life back together. After all, at the moment, you are still officially listed as dead," stated Robertson.

Following a formal welcome from the senior commanding officer of Joint Base Andrews, the three comrades climbed into a base vehicle and were driven away to the Malcolm Grow Medical Clinics and Surgery Center, where he would stay as he acclimatized to the States once again.

The next few weeks were difficult for Nathan. He voluntarily agreed to be restricted to base until such time as the medical staff felt he was ready for the outside world. Senior officers gave Dwayne special permission to spend as much time with Nathan as his friend wanted. Between specialist appointments, follow-up surgeries, physical therapy, and daily counseling sessions, the two long-term friends spent their time engrossed in watching sport, so Nathan could catch up on his beloved football and hockey, taking in a few new films on a projection screen that the base set up especially for them, walks in the outdoors around the base and generally engaging in activities that helped him become familiar with a normal life again.

Each and every day, Nathan asked about Lisa and Charlotte; when would he be allowed to speak to them, when would they be given permission to come and see him, what had happened to them since he was captured? Despite doing well in the eyes of those treating him, or so they thought as he acted and told them what they wanted to hear, Nathan found it impossible to hide his frustration and anger about the lack of information regarding his family. Dwayne knew exactly why they gave him the runaround, and eventually decided that he deserved to know the truth. Sitting outside in the sun one afternoon, against professional advice and his own better judgment, Dwayne finally told Nathan what he wanted to know.

"Hey, man, I know the docs don't want you to deal with this yet, but Nath, I think you need to know the truth. There is a reason why Lisa wasn't there to meet you, why she hasn't come to see you and why they won't let you see her... she got remarried about four months ago. You gotta understand, buddy, she thought you were dead... we all did!"

Dwayne might as well have put a gun to Nathan's head and pulled the trigger. He'd feared she might have moved on, but never did he consider she would have met someone new and remarried. What little resolve and stability he had built up mentally came crashing down in an instant. He could never forgive them for leaving him behind, but to now have cost him his family and not even told him about it was the final straw. He immediately set himself the goal of gaining approval to return to normal life as quickly as possible, so he could finally speak to Lisa and see his daughter.

Nathan worked single-mindedly toward his objective. Dwayne confessed to having told him the truth and despite the psychologist's initial concerns, Nathan tirelessly did everything he could to prove to them that he was "alright" with the news and accepted it; after all, what else could he do? He pushed hard to recover from his physical injuries—whether it was with an eye specialist retraining his sight or in the gym rebuilding his muscles and ligaments. He became the model soldier who'd fought through untold adversity and come out the other side a better man. The truth was vastly different. He held no malice toward Dwayne as an individual, he accepted he would never have retreated had he known, but he despised the rest of the military that left him behind. He also hated the country that had abandoned him and cost him his family; he vowed to get even one day, how and when he didn't know, but there would be retribution for all he'd suffered.

Eventually, Nathan convinced those in charge to release him. He was officially allowed to retire from the Marine Corps, and their parting gift was to provide him with enough money to buy himself a small house in Washington. They also arranged for him to finally see his family… or so he thought. Lisa agreed to allow him to come to her house, where Nathan assumed he would finally see his daughter. Dwayne drove him there that morning and told him he'd wait in the car and to shout if he needed him. Nathan had never been as scared as he was when he walked up those wooden steps and knocked on the door. A minute later, Lisa answered; she looked as beautiful as ever, and the old Nathan suddenly began to force his way to the surface. He was invited in and took a moment to look around the new house where she now lived. It was bigger than the one they had bought, and a tear forced its way out when he saw pictures of Charlotte on the wall of the stairs. Having sat in the living room, Lisa told him all that had happened.

"Nathan, I don't really know what to say. They told me you were dead about two days after the firefight in the village. I was absolutely devastated. I had to stop teaching for a while, and I really struggled. You must know I hoped for many months that the information was wrong, that you were actually alive, but in the end I had to accept the reality. I eventually dealt with all your affairs and the finality of it was soul-destroying. Slowly, as the months passed, I had to get my life back together, if only for Charlotte."

"Where is Charlotte, I can't wait to see her?" replied Nathan, the first time he'd genuinely felt excitement over something.

"She's not here, Nathan. Please, let me explain. I met Richard just over a year ago. He was the business accountant for one of my friends and she kind of put us together. We got on straight away and moved in together several months later. He has a son from a previous marriage, Julian, who adores his little sister. We got married about four months ago. I know this isn't easy to hear, but Charlotte and I are happy in our new life, and I hope one day that you'll be able to accept that and possibly even be happy for us. I let Richard take Charlotte with him today. She is going to need time, Nathan. She will not recognize you, and she has finally got used to Richard as her adopted father. Right now, I don't want to confuse her. I absolutely want you to have a relationship with her, but I have to do what is best for Charlotte at this early age. I will find a way for you to see her in the next few weeks, and I am quite happy for you to spend a little time with her over the next few years, but I beg you, for her sake, to be patient. As she gets older and can understand what happened, I hope you will have the close relationship you want and deserve…"

Nathan swallowed down his rage. The realist in him knew that Lisa had no option but to move on with her life. He'd told himself that numerous times, but accepting it was something entirely different. He'd set his heart on seeing his daughter, and to have that ripped away was the final indignity. Losing Lisa was bad enough, to be told he'd have limited contact with his own daughter was catastrophic. He knew "a little time" translated to hardly at all. Everything had now been taken away from him… everything.

The two of them told Dwayne they were okay, and he left them to it. They talked for a couple of hours, Lisa genuinely wanting to know what he'd been through. She was as compassionate as ever, and broke down in tears multiple times. There were moments when Nathan wanted to show his real feelings, his hostilities about all that had been ripped from him, but much like he had in captivity, he remained true to his "act", the persona he wanted everyone to see. It was soon time for Charlotte and Richard to come home, and Nathan agreed to call it a day. Dwayne picked him up and despite all his offers of wanting to keep his friend company, that it wouldn't do any good for him to be alone after such an emotional day, Nathan assured him that he'd be alright.

As the days and weeks passed, two very different men began to take shape. There was the Nathan Profit that he wanted everyone to see. That man worked hard at his rehab, accepted what had happened—both in Afghanistan and with his family —spoke positively about the future, and was "genuinely" trying to be the best man he could be. In private, there was the other Nathan Profit. That Nathan was filled with venom and hatred toward his country and everyone in the military. He was in a spiral of depression and suicidal thoughts, and drank to excess each night. This part of him spent hours every evening, all evening, plotting and scheming how he'd make everyone pay. This was the real Nathan Profit.

It was this double life that finally delivered his plan for revenge. He would continue to be two different men. There would be the Nathan that everyone saw, a man pulling himself out of the most horrendous, unimaginable situation. He would retrain, get a new job, and create a life that people would be proud of him for doing. It would be an existence without questions, without suspicion. His alter ego, his private Mr. Hyde to his public-facing Dr. Jekyll, would be the wronged man out to extract his revenge, both on those directly responsible for what happened to him in Afghanistan and the people of the decadent, disgusting country that deserted him.

To earn the money to finance his intentions, Nathan obtained permission from the highest echelons of the armed forces to sell his story to the press, although everything had to be officially cleared first. In their eyes, it was the ultimate positive publicity, as long as it was dealt with correctly. Here was a man who was subjected to horrific torture by terrorists, the enemies of the West, a direct and unquestionable example of why the War on Terror was so important. He gave interviews to every newspaper who would talk to him, local and national, and also appeared on radio and even a few television shows. He took it just far enough to make himself financially very comfortable, but without becoming such a well-known figure that it would affect his "other" plans. It amazed Nathan how much money he was able to earn in the process, that he was paid a substantial amount just for retelling his story. When added to the remainder of the large payoff that he received when he left the marines, Nathan had all the cash he would ever need.

With his financial situation now secure, Nathan planned the next step. He needed to be seen to be doing good, but at the same time to have the opportunity to deliver the sort of retribution and punishment he knew certain people deserved. The answer was quite simple in the end. Given he already possessed a considerable medical background from his seven years at L.S.U., Nathan decided to retrain and refresh his knowledge, so he could take up the perfect position for a man with his intentions. It would be a job where he could help those in genuine need and provide merciless payback to those who warranted it. Nathan had made his decision; he would join the Fire Service as an emergency medic… a First Responder!

CHAPTER 4

The plan that Nathan had formulated wasn't the sort of scheme that could be enacted within a week or two; in military terminology, it would be described as "playing the long game." He knew his existing experience and knowledge would stand him in good stead when it came to his firefighter paramedic application, but still he made some informal approaches to a couple of local fire station captains to test whether his assumptions were correct. They both confirmed that once he'd gotten his medical training up to date, his application to the Fire Academy would be a formality. The only possible question mark they both raised was whether Nathan would be physically fit enough to pass the fireman aspect of the role.

Throughout his five years of service, the marines had always afforded Nathan special dispensation to maintain his medical qualifications, which meant he had all the foundational knowledge required to be a paramedic. It was an unusual situation, but both his former Lieutenant (Robertson) and his Captain (Anderson) saw the benefit of having such a medically qualified staff sergeant. The length of his incarceration meant he would still need to study hard and catch up with the latest treatments, but it was literally a case of refreshing his mind and taking the relevant exams. He thrilled his counselors with his career plan, and they were able to help cut through the red-tape to expedite his re-education. Over the next few months, Nathan studied hard and also began to push his body to ensure he could manage the physically demanding job. As he approached the time to take his paramedic exams, Nathan submitted his official application to join the fire service. As predicted, he was accepted immediately and swiftly enrolled in the Washington, D.C. Fire & E.M.S. Training Academy.

The training process to become a fireman could take anywhere between three and twelve months, but Nathan's previous military knowledge and experience were invaluable, and it enabled him to quickly get ahead of the curve. By the time he was three months into his training, Nathan's body was more or less healed from all the abuse it had suffered in Afghanistan. There were days when he found it more of a struggle than others, but he always knew that would be the case. As he pushed his physical and mental abilities to the limit, he also worked hard to create the personality and external image that he felt everyone needed to see. He was the perfect student— always willing, always proactive, and always enthusiastic—and he made sure he helped his fellow new recruits whenever possible. Everyone loved Nathan, whether it was another trainee going through the process or his tutors and senior officers at the training academy.

Outside his single-minded pursuit of the perfect career to carry out his plans, Nathan did everything he could to create a private life that matched the one he wanted to professionally portray. His house was always clean and presentable, and very much the sort of abode that a single bachelor in his mid-thirties would have, aside from a number of pictures of Charlotte that were dotted around the place. His love for his daughter was about the only genuine thing he showed to people, but it also served as an inspirational reminder to him as to why he'd chosen the path he had. The positive leaps he'd made encouraged Lisa to feel a little more comfortable with Nathan seeing his daughter. She had laid down some fairly strict rules, such as he couldn't see her on his own—Lisa always had to be present—and it had to be under the disguise of "mommy catching up with her friend" rather than Charlotte seeing her dad. He hated it, even more than he realized when he agreed to the conditions, and it only strengthened his resolve when it came to his plan and desired outcomes.

Nathan would have been happy to work hard during the day at his training and simply spend the evenings alone as he concentrated on the finer points of what he needed to do in the months that followed. He'd always been a great team player in the marines, whether it was on or off duty, and he was usually the life and soul of any social gathering. The new Nathan often made excuses that he needed to study or had other commitments when he was asked to join the other trainees for a night out, but he knew he had to take part occasionally, if only to maintain the image he was trying to establish. If he did join them, he made sure he only had a couple of beers, so there was no risk that he might inadvertently say something he shouldn't. It never ceased to surprise him how much effort it took when you had to fake that you were having fun.

Aside from his associates in the training academy, Nathan also maintained regular contact with Dwayne. He felt comfortable enough with him to let Dwayne witness more of his personal struggles than he did anyone else. He never let his guard down, but allowed his best friend to see a few more truthful slivers of the real Nathan Profit—the man who found the limited contact with his daughter difficult, the man who still missed his wife and family, and the man who still had the "occasional" nightmare about his time in Afghanistan. Nathan made sure that he never divulged too much or anything that Dwayne might feel obligated to tell his councilor or senior trainers about, but his best friend became his sole outlet to be just a little more real than he was with everyone else.

After seven months of hard work, Nathan Profit graduated from the fire service training academy. He had already passed all the latest paramedic exams and was now ready to begin his new career. Despite his extensive background and top-of-the-class grades, Nathan would still have to go through the usual probation period that any firefighter was required to complete, an initial phase that could last anywhere between six months and two years. Lucas, Lisa, and Dwayne were all at his graduation ceremony, and for once Nathan didn't have to fake his reaction as he was genuinely thrilled to have completed his training. When all the pomp and pageantry had finished, Nathan and Dwayne celebrated that evening with a meal and a couple of drinks. As they sat at the table, his long-time friend found it difficult to hide the admiration he felt at witnessing Nathan's monumental achievement.

"I gotta say, Nath, I am really proud of you," confessed Dwayne. "I can still see you when you stepped off that plane at Andrews and I don't mind admitting it, I was genuinely concerned about what the future would hold for you. I have seen some seriously injured dudes, but man, I don't know anyone who has gone through what you have, and I doubt I ever will. I will always regret what happened, I don't think I'll ever forgive..."

Nathan interrupted before he could finish. "You have to try, Dwayne. It wasn't your call, you know that, and as a soldier, you have to follow the orders you are given. I never once blamed you during the time I was a prisoner, and I still don't blame you now. I know it's easier said than done, but one day you will have to forgive yourself."

"I'm not sure if I ever will... but it certainly makes it a little easier to see what has become of you. I know there were some dark days there, Nath, especially after you first saw Lisa, but what you have done is nothing short of remarkable. My friend, the retired soldier who went to hell and back, now a fully qualified firefighter paramedic," declared Dwayne proudly.

He raised his drink and the two glasses chinked loudly. Although he wouldn't dare say it, Dwayne was genuinely surprised Nathan was still alive. It had nothing to do with what he'd suffered in Afghanistan—he had nothing but admiration for what his friend had survived in the Middle East—but he saw him in the days and weeks after he'd finally met Lisa, and no matter how hard he had tried to hide it, Dwayne knew Nathan really suffered. He'd popped round to visit him a few times, and seen Nathan passed out on the sofa with bottles of whiskey and rum scattered all around. He didn't need to be a clinical psychologist to know that the secret insights he'd observed through the window were those of a man very close to giving up. It was one of the reasons he kept close contact with Nathan, hoping if he finally reached rock bottom and considered taking his life, that maybe he could stop it. There were a couple of times he almost confessed to Nathan what he'd been privy to, but he clung onto the hope that his buddy would find a way through his self-inflicted torture, and eventually he did.

That evening was the first time Nathan had felt anything resembling normality since he returned from the Middle East. It reminded him how the two of them had often gone out together on similar nighttime excursions when they were in the marines. Following their meal, they went to a bar and played a few games of pool. Nathan even found the urge to chuck some change in the jukebox and whack on a few Classic Rock hits from the eighties. Dwayne was more of a dance music fan, and just rolled his eyes as the guitar-based tunes rolled out of the speakers.

"Nath, we have got to do something about your taste in music, man. This isn't retro, it's prehistoric. The ol' Neolithic hunter-gatherers used to go out and kill their mammoth or saber-tooth tiger, then stop at the record shop on their way home and pick up that latest album from this group," teased Dwayne.

"Dude, I can't help it if your musical taste is limited to a drum-machine and a record played backward," quipped Nathan.

"When we get you back out there, my friend, if you don't update your tunes, the only ladies interested in you will come wrapped in bandages and live in a decorated box; your music is so old even an Egyptian mummy would consider you out of date," laughed Dwayne as he potted another ball.

Nathan had already decided he would allow himself one night of peace, a lone evening in the wilderness of his new existence, where he would let the man he used to be come up for air. He did have a good time with Dwayne, and there was the very briefest of seconds where he contemplated that maybe there was another way, but suddenly a photo in Lisa's house, one that featured Charlotte sitting with Richard, entered his mind and any good intention evaporated like the fires he would help put out in the coming months. Eventually, their evening came to an end and the two men stood outside the bar to bid each other good night, exactly like they had done so many times in the past.

"Good luck with your first few days. You don't need it, but I'll say it anyway. Just do me a favor, try not to get yourself cooked like one of your charcoal styled BBQ burgers," urged Dwayne.

"There ain't nothing wrong with my BBQ cooking, thank you very much," insisted Nathan.

"No, nothing at all, as long as you like your food comparable to the extinguished embers of a campfire," laughed Dwayne.

"I'll be all good. I'm ready. It's time to move forward," Nathan assured him, just without explaining what he truly meant.

The two friends hugged and went their separate ways. As he walked along, Nathan looked up at the stars, something he'd often done with Lisa as they sat on the two-person swing in his old backyard. Most people would probably have some doubts about what they were about to embark on, but not Nathan. He told himself there probably wasn't a man alive who was more committed to a task than he was. With the groundwork done, it was now time to put his plan into action.

Nathan spent the weekend making sure everything was in order for his big day. The old, judiciously prepared marine reappeared as he double-checked that everything was as it should be. He woke up bright and early on Monday morning and went for a run to clear his mind. After a shower and breakfast, he chucked his well-packed kit bag on the rear seat and drove to the station. There were thirty-six fire stations in the D.C. area, and the head office had assigned Nathan to one that was located near the center of the district.

He was the only graduate from his class at that particular firehouse, and he was greeted upon his arrival by the station's senior officer, Captain Geoff Mitchell. At fifty-nine years of age, the captain was at the backend of his career, but he proudly informed Nathan during his induction meeting that his passion for the job was every bit as fierce as the day he walked in as a new recruit. His piercing green eyes lit up as he told Nathan some of the station's history. Despite his intended plans, Nathan warmed quickly to the 6'2 station captain with the bald head, dark gray beard, and slightly paunchy figure. He was then handed over to his Lieutenant, John Spencer, a 6'0 man in his early fifties with short gray hair, an average build and an imposing, deep voice. It was his job to show Nathan around the rest of the station, and to get him up to speed on procedures, expectations, the staff rotation, and the day-to-day running of the building.

Spencer next introduced Nathan to Peter Adams, a 6'0, forty-year-old man with a large build, brownish hair and a beard, who was the driver engineer for the truck he would be working from. The captain had decided that Nathan should learn the ropes by shadowing one of the firefighters, and he picked Doug O'Brien to help the station's newest member. Right from the outset, it was obvious that Doug was a vibrant, larger-than-life personality; it would be difficult to visually miss the 6'2, athletically muscular man with short flame-red hair, but it was impossible to ignore the infectious, rather loud fireman even when you were in a different room. The other two members of Nathan's team were Clarissa James, a forty-two-year-old, slim built, 5'8 lady with long brown hair, warm brown eyes and a ferocious mentality, and Tom Fryer, a thirty-eight-year-old, athletic, 6'1 fireman with short blond hair, blue eyes and a real swagger.

It took Nathan a few days to begin finding a comfortable level around his vastly more experienced colleagues. It was an unusual feeling for him because he had become so used to being the one that showed the rookie marines what to do when they first joined his squad. The captain clearly knew his staff because the pairing of Nathan and Doug worked really well right from the start. The initial few days were rather quiet, but toward the end of the first week, there was a major callout to a M.V.A.—Motor Vehicle Accident—that involved two cars and a van. There were minor injuries to two of the four victims, but Doug and Tom had to cut two patients from the second car. They watched, almost in awe, as the rookie firefighter paramedic swooped into action and dealt with the situation like he'd been doing it for years. Nathan handled the situation perfectly and was roundly applauded by everyone when they returned to the station. As first incidents went, it wasn't the most difficult, but it proved his previous experience would serve him well going forward.

"You're going to go far, son," Capt. Mitchell told him just before he went off-shift that night.

Over the weekend, Dwayne stopped by for a few hours and told Nathan that he was thrilled that the capital's newest first responder had passed his initial test with flying colors.

"You're made for this, Nath, honestly… you were a great marine, but I have a feeling you're going to be an even better paramedic. I am willing to bet you're gonna wish you had taken this career path years ago, instead of sweating your balls off with me in Afghanistan," jested Dwayne as they sat on Nathan's porch with a beer in hand.

Nathan ensured he did everything exactly by the book during his first few weeks. He attended numerous callouts, and treated everyone correctly and perfectly according to their needs. The reputation he knew he so badly needed, the one that would mask his true intentions, was quickly established and now it was just a matter of time. A few weeks later, he was presented with his first opportunity to punish the sort of scum that the decadent country he now detested had created.

The team were tasked with assisting an injured man who'd badly broken his leg. It was the sort of incident that would normally be dealt with by an ambulance, but there had been multiple other emergency calls in the previous half-hour, so dispatch had asked the fire crew to attend one of the more run-of-the-mill situations. The emergency services call center advised that the police officer who called it in had quietly asked her to let the attending E.M.T. know that the patient in question was a well-known drug dealer who'd previously been accused, investigated, and charged with selling a variety of illegal drugs to underage kids, although a jury acquitted him after a trial. Before the engine even left the building, Nathan instantly decided that the man needed to be taught a lesson, justifying his upcoming actions of causing suffering to someone who themselves caused suffering to others.

Aware the man was already in considerable pain and trying to delay their arrival, Nathan's first intervention was to suggest an alternate route, a short-cut, to Peter that should have gotten them there quicker. His driving colleague agreed with the idea, but unlike Nathan, Peter didn't know about the major roadworks that had started just three days earlier along the suggested new route. It added nearly fifteen minutes to their journey and Nathan swiftly offered his "deepest apologies", but

Peter told him not to worry about it; he agreed his suggestion was a good one, and it was just unfortunate timing that it coincided with the utility companies digging up the road. As he mentioned… how was Nathan to know?

When they arrived, they found a Caucasian man in his mid-thirties lying flat on his back in the middle of a basketball court with a seriously broken leg. As Clarissa and Tom gathered information from witnesses about what had happened—basically, the man had landed awkwardly as he showed off—Nathan made sure everyone saw his professional, caring facade. He spoke tenderly and politely to the man, asking him how he'd fell, where it hurt and all the other expected questions that any well-trained medic would need answers to. During his conversation with the patient, Nathan couldn't avoid hearing a couple of people whispering in the background that he should leave the "parasite" to suffer. He couldn't do that, not directly anyway, so he quickly formulated an alternative approach.

Nathan asked everyone to back up and give him plenty of space, then continued to assess the leg until he saw Clarissa preoccupied with taking detailed notes from the man's friend. That only left Tom, and Nathan quickly distracted his other colleague by sending him to the engine for some equipment, specifically a couple of splints. He was now alone with the patient and presented with the opportunity he had been waiting for. Still sounding caring and sympathetic, Nathan delivered his prognosis.

"Well, you've definitely broken your tibia. It looks like you have a displaced transverse fracture, which means it's a straight break, but the bone is misaligned. I'm sorry to say, I will need to straighten that before I put you in a splint," he informed the man.

Nodding nervously, the patient gave his consent for Nathan to correct the misaligned bone. A sudden rush of adrenaline thundered through Nathan's body as he prepared to "treat" the man. He did indeed have a transverse fracture, that part of Nathan's diagnosis was absolutely correct, but the bone had simply snapped and not moved; there was no need for the bone to be straightened at all. Acting quickly before his window of opportunity closed, Nathan injected the man in his thigh with a syringe of saline water, not the anesthetic he'd promised, then having gripped his victim's ankle and knee in each hand, he twisted the broken leg, so the bone actually did displace. The man let out a blood-curdling howl, and both Clarissa and Tom came rushing over to see if Nathan needed help.

"It's a displaced tibia fracture; I've almost got it back in line, I just need to move it a little more," he told everyone.

With the bone now actually out of place, Nathan "corrected" the displacement and put the bones back in line, which caused even more agonizing screams from the man.

"I'll just give you a little more anesthetic to better numb the leg before we splint you up," he said to the man.

This time, he gave him the anesthetic that should have been administered at the start. As they waited for the ambulance that would take the man to the hospital, Nathan put his leg in a splint, only instead of securing it correctly, he set it so that the bone was actually being pulled apart, which caused continual pain for the man despite the anesthetic. He looked down, and the expression of agony on the man's face gave him an immense feeling of satisfaction. When the ambulance arrived at the scene, it only had a driver and a single medic in the back; their colleague had stayed at the hospital to finish admitting their previous patient who was seriously injured, knowing the next pickup was just a broken leg that a firefighter paramedic had already attended to.

Nathan's original plan had been to correct the splint just before they handed the patient over to the ambulance team. With his shift almost over and presented with the chance to continue his victim's suffering, Nathan offered to help out the ambulance crew by going with them in the vehicle to the hospital; the medics were grateful for the gesture and happily accepted. Just before they reached the hospital, he craftily created a situation where the stretcher suddenly moved—he'd previously made sure he wasn't the one that secured it before they left—and used that as an excuse for the splint having "drifted" out of place. He swiftly adjusted it, and by the time the E.R. department had taken over the patient, everything was exactly as it should be.

That night, Nathan felt invigorated, the thrill of his actions that afternoon providing him with more gratification than even he'd expected. He had proved to himself that he could do what was needed to those he deemed unworthy. It had also given him the inspiration and motivation to begin work on the other, more dangerous part of his plan—to exact his revenge on those who left him for dead in Afghanistan. He had always been rather tech-savvy, and now he put that knowledge to good use as he began searching the dark web for contacts who could provide him with the information, the means, and the opportunity to unleash his wrath.

CHAPTER 5

It was a tense few days for Nathan following the hostile treatment he dished out to the drug dealer. He was confident that by the time the hospital took over the criminal's care, there were no signs of his mistreatment nor any suspicion from the man himself that his first responder had done anything untoward. However, Nathan had also been in the military long enough to know that things could go wrong, even with the best of planning. Sometimes you could forget or overlook something, other times it could be because someone acted differently than you'd assumed or there is evidence from a completely unexpected source. All he could do was act normal and carry on like he'd provided the best care possible, and hope he was as good as he thought he was.

He arrived at work the next day and simply went about his business. He didn't ask any unusual questions to probe whether there had been any questionable feedback, and made a point to focus on what came next rather than proudly look back on what he'd done. The only moment of anxiety was when Clarissa inquired how much anesthetic Nathan had initially given the patient, due to the fact he was still in quite a bit of pain when he'd first manipulated the displaced fracture. He gave a figure at the lower end of the suggested amount, and quickly headed off any further questions by admitting he should probably have administered a stronger dose. Aside from that small private query, he was again praised for his work ethic, his swift diagnosis of a difficult fracture, and his dedication to helping anyone who needed it, regardless of whether they were a good person or not.

"At the end of the day, we all took the Hippocratic Oath. He wasn't a good man, but that doesn't come into it," lied Nathan during the daily team meeting that morning.

As the days passed, there was no negative blow-back from the incident. Given he was a probationer, Nathan was certain that his captain would have pulled him up straight away had the hospital reached out with any fears about possible or probable mistreatment. Feeling both happy and increasingly bold, Nathan reminded himself that he needed to be cautious. Over-confidence was often the reason that the police caught most criminals, and though he certainly didn't consider himself a felon, he knew no one would understand his actions... or so he initially thought.

During the evenings, he was increasingly spending his time buried inside the dark web. It was not a place for the faint-hearted, and Nathan knew it was frequented by people with all sorts of pursuits and ideals that ranged from questionable to downright awful. Before he delved too deeply into the lawless frontier of perversion and sadistic brutality, some of the more reasonable hackers in the less disturbing chat rooms had given him some advice on how to increase his already substantial security and anonymity. Now supremely assured that it would be extremely difficult to track his actions, Nathan abandoned any previous hesitations he had and surfed with impunity wherever he wanted.

He spent the majority of his time in anti-capitalist and anti-American chat rooms. A large percentage of them were a hotbed of terrorist fundamentalism, and though he rabidly hated his country for abandoning him, he hadn't gone so far down the rabbit hole that he now saw the merits of religious ideology. He made a promise that if he uncovered talk of a terrorist atrocity on ordinary American people, he would find a way to stop it happening. If their intention was to attack the Pentagon or a military installation, they could do their worst. As he became more familiar with the dark web, he found the sort of discussions that he wanted to be part of. There were two rooms in particular that he conversed in regularly. One was a "passionate to the point of fury" outlet for people who thought that America had passed the point of no return when it came to morals and decency. He knew as little about those in the chat room as they knew about him, but it seemed to be a mixture of surfers who yearned for a return to old-school values and people who were hell-bent on wiping out all vestiges of decadence that had become the norm.

He didn't realize it, but the constant brainwashing from Khalid and his fellow abusers had actually affected his once very open-minded view of the world. Nathan had never had any issues with anyone's religion, race, color, creed, sex, or sexuality, but now he found himself feeling revulsion and agreement with those who were very much opposed to anything connected to diversity and inclusion. He felt no shame as he agreed with ranting discussions that two years ago he would have found abhorrent.

The other chat room he favored centered very much on discussions that were anti-American. It wasn't so much about the moral illness that was sweeping across the country—"The libertarian virus that had spread into every part of the nation." —but more connected with how American politicians and its armed forces seem to feel it was their right to impose their values on the rest of the world. It was very anti-military, and this struck a real chord with Nathan. He was extremely careful in his conversations not to give anything away that would allow someone to connect him with the public interviews he'd previously given. There were numerous ex-military people who congregated in the chat room; no one gave any specifics, but their knowledge, experiences, and insights were clearly those of people who'd previously served their country. What they all shared was a hatred of everything that America had done in recent decades, and similar negative experiences that left them wanting to make someone pay for something. With every passing week, Nathan felt more comfortable and more relaxed about his views of the country and those who abandoned him, the people he regularly conversed with simply inflating his already hostile outlook.

A few users regularly referred to a bar called Through the Looking Glass that was located on the outskirts of D.C. It was a tavern frequented by many people with "different" and "majority displeasing" views of the world. He was told it wasn't some sort of secret society, just a place where the discussions could offend those with a rather delicate persuasion. The bar even hosted a stand-up comedy night every two weeks, and the humor on display was risqué and near-the-knuckle, to say the least. Nathan decided he would make a point of going there a few times to see what he thought of the place, although he certainly didn't publicly say that in the chat room.

He continued to forge the perfect persona in his day job, and his entirely planned "good work ethic" saw him regularly praised by his colleagues. As they learned more about what happened to him in Afghanistan, the specific details and events leaving everyone aghast, his fellow team members became increasingly impressed with his conduct. About three weeks after his altercation with the drug dealer, the team were called out to a serious M.V.A. that offered Nathan the perfect set of circumstances to prove himself and to cement, once and for all, the public-facing image he was trying to craft.

The incident involved three cars that had collided head-on when one of the vehicles had a blown-out front tire and careered across two lanes into the oncoming traffic traveling in the opposite direction. The ambulances were already on their way, but they desperately needed fire crews at the scene to cut injured victims from the wreckage. Upon their arrival, Doug, Peter, Tom, and Lt. Spencer—the latter coming along because it was an "all hands on deck" incident—assessed the situation as Nathan and Clarissa collected up all the medical equipment they would need. The lone occupant of the car that lost control was already dead—killed either on impact or when the car rolled over several times and slammed into a bank—but the people in the other two cars were still alive. When they had finished making their plan of action, Lt. Spencer came over to Nathan.

"Errr, Nathan, we have a bit of a situation here. I know you are committed to your medical oath and your responsibilities, one hundred percent, no question, but there is an aspect of this callout I need to quickly discuss with you before you get to work," said his senior officer.

For a few seconds, Nathan's heart sank to the pit of his stomach. Was Spencer about to tell him that one of the cars belonged to someone he knew. As far as he could see, he didn't recognize any of the vehicles, but maybe Lisa, Dwayne or, God forbid, Charlotte were traveling with someone else. He began to panic, and Lt. Spencer could see the concern rapidly spread across his face.

"Nathan, don't worry, as far as I'm aware, it doesn't involve anyone you know," confirmed Spencer.

What could it be? If he'd had half an hour to mull over various possibilities, it was unlikely he'd have come up with the right one.

"There are two people, a male and a female, in the car that was hit first. They have some serious lacerations, possibly some broken bones, and I would expect some head trauma. My hesitation isn't with the people in that vehicle, it's the family in the third car. The vehicle's front is badly smashed, and Tom and Doug are already in the process of cutting the occupants free. There is a family of four in there, a male, a female, a teenage boy, and a girl around twelve..."

Nathan was still rather bemused; nothing that the Lieutenant had told him required any sort of special preparation or seemed to necessitate the extra intervention.

"...the reason I pulled you up before letting you get to work is because of their nationality. Nathan, they're from Afghanistan!"

Now it all made sense! Both the station captain and lieutenant had been fully briefed about Nathan's past, and both had seen his medical records... including the psychiatric reports. He knew there was nothing in there that would prompt direct concerns should Nathan have to deal with someone from Afghanistan, but he also knew that his superiors had to be sure he could handle the situation before allowing him to carry out his job.

"No one would think any less of you if this is too much. From what they have just told me, the father is an ex-interpreter who was granted asylum two years ago when people made death threats against him and his family. I assure you... he is not ex-Taliban or Al-Qaeda. However, it would be remiss of me not to ensure you are okay with this. If you need to, you can attend to the less serious injuries in the first car, and Clarissa can treat the Afghan family. If she has any questions, she can shout over to you. It is your call, Nathan; there will be no comeback regardless of how you want to handle this," assured Spencer.

Deep down, Nathan would have loved to have inflicted serious harm on the father and his family. As far as he was concerned, all four of them could be left to bleed out in their vehicle. That would never be allowed, so for a few seconds he contemplated whether there was a way he could use the situation to make them pay for what he'd been through. No matter how enraged he was inside and how strong his urge for retribution, Nathan knew his exuberance and overwhelming emotional state may lead him to make an obvious mistake that would raise questions. He also knew if he refused to treat them, despite the assurances from his Lieutenant, that it would irrevocably ruin the image he'd created.

"I appreciate the honesty, and I am very grateful for the offer to leave this to others, but I am a paramedic and this is my job," he strongly reiterated. "This man didn't torture me, and this man didn't kill members of my team. If anything, his actions probably saved marines. If they are the most seriously injured and that is where I am needed, then let me get to work. Where they come from makes no difference."

Nathan felt physically sick, and he had to almost swallow the vomit that began to rise in his throat. Even speaking the words made him want to gag, but this was about the bigger picture. Besides, maybe he'd find out more about them and possibly be able to dish out some richly deserved punishment at a later date.

As the other members of his crew got to work cutting the injured victims from the two seriously wrecked cars, Nathan and Clarissa began treating the wounded. Every second was a struggle for the ex-marine. Just looking at the man and hearing his accent made Nathan want to end his life and that of his family. During a pause as he waited for the next person to be freed, he imagined how good he'd feel to slit the throats of the two children and the wife, right in front of the man as he watched, powerless to intervene, before he then put his hands around the man's throat and squeezed the life out of him. No matter how much he yearned to carry out his fantasy, it would have to remain just that.

Nathan's treatment of the Afghan family was exemplary. At one point, it looked like the older male child wouldn't make it. He stopped breathing and was bleeding out. Nathan not only resuscitated him, but his swift action with the wound saved the child's life. He also noticed the mother appeared to have a serious internal injury and contemplated "overlooking" it. Even the best, most experienced paramedic could have misdiagnosed the signs, and he was sure no one would think any less of him were she to die from it, but he didn't want even the tiniest negativity to be directed at him. He acted quickly, did what he could and immediately alerted the ambulance teams who were also attending the scene.

It was a difficult, arduous, and unpleasant accident, but the six people hit by the oncoming car all survived. That evening, Captain Mitchell gathered the whole team.

"Everyone, I have here in my hand one of those special bottles of red wine from my favorite Napa vineyard…"

A resounding "Oooo…" came from the rest of the team.

"Alright, cut the sarcasm. As most of you know, I only dish one of these out when someone has performed way above and beyond or done something that is truly special. Tonight, I'm pleased to award this bottle to Nathan Profit…"

Everyone clapped and cheered.

"…who performed his duties like a true hero this afternoon. Nathan, today you saw a man and his family in dire need of your help, and not their nationality. You could have taken the easy route and treated the others, but you didn't. In recognition of your actions, I present this extremely delicious bottle of wine to you… and you'll get your name added to our little unofficial Board of Honor in the mess room. Well done, son."

Nathan stepped forward, shook his hand, and took the wine. He thanked everyone and made a point to say that he'd merely done his job, and during the entire two-minute speech, he told them what they needed to hear. In truth, the whole situation infuriated him beyond belief. He was extremely annoyed that he hadn't been able to carry out his true intentions, and that he'd effectively been pressured into doing the right thing regardless of how strongly he felt about it inside.

He fumed the entire drive home and spent half of it talking to himself as he complained and vented at what had taken place that afternoon. When he got home, he slumped in his chair and remained there for nearly an hour, lost in his own thoughts, and intermittently staring at the photos of his daughter on the wall. Eventually, it all boiled over, and he picked up the bottle of wine and hurled it at the wall. The glass shattered everywhere, and the red wine splashed all over the wall. Due to its color, it resembled a blood spatter pattern.

"What a shame it's not that Afghan's blood that is sprayed everywhere," he muttered to himself.

He tried hard to lay the day's events to rest and having cooked himself a meal, Nathan sat down to watch the television. He switched on the news, and one of the main stories contained footage from a violent gun battle between the Los Angeles Police and two closely affiliated gangs. The worst of it obviously wasn't shown, but seeing the thuggish trash from the L.A. ghettos only worsened Nathan's mood. It was all the incentive he required to reaffirm his commitment to doing what he thought needed to be done. He wouldn't take reckless risks, that would serve no purpose, but going forward, those that had it coming would get their just deserts!

Early the next week, the fire crew were called out to a local high-school where a scientific experiment had suddenly gone wrong and caused a fire that threatened to quickly get out of control. The engine was there within minutes, and it didn't take Doug, Tom, and Nathan very long to put it out. As they were tidying up their equipment and getting ready to leave, one of the teachers came rushing over in a blind panic.

"Help, please, are any of you medically qualified or a paramedic? One of our students is having a serious allergic reaction in the canteen," she asked breathlessly.

Nathan grabbed his bag and told her, "I'm a paramedic, show me the way, quickly. Doug, come and give me a hand."

The three of them jogged through the main entrance, and the woman directed them to the mess hall. In one corner, there was a group of students standing around two other teachers who were kneeling either side of a youngster who was clearly in distress.

Moving the gawking teenagers aside, Nathan asked, "What happened? Does anyone know what he's allergic to and what he's swallowed?"

From what he was told, it became immediately apparent that the student on the floor was the school bully, although it wasn't said in such a direct manner, and that he'd physically stolen two sandwiches from a girl who was unable to stand up for herself. In his haste to consume something that wasn't his, the boy was totally unaware that the contents of the sandwich included traces of sesame seeds. Within minutes, he'd gone into anaphylactic shock and the staff could only look on, almost helpless, while the student laid on the floor, coughing and seriously fighting for breath. He had only experienced such severe symptoms once and had no medication of his own. As Doug made sure they had all the necessary information from the bullied girl and teachers, Nathan discretely prepared the EpiPen injection in the bag. However, instead of treating the patient, he placed it in a tucked-away pocket in his med-kit, one that was unlikely to be looked at straight away.

"Doug, where the fuck is the EpiPen, it's supposed to be in this pouch?" screamed Nathan.

His mentor came over and looked through the bag himself and found nothing.

"Jesus, it's not in here! I'll have to run out and grab the other one from the second med-kit. Do what you can until I get back!" replied Doug in a panic.

Nathan kneeled down and showed pretend concern for the boy, telling him to remain calm and that help would be there soon. The abject fear in the boy's eyes and the pain he was suffering provided Nathan with immense gratification and pleasure. He pondered whether to help the boy at all, the chance of his situation becoming fatal growing with every second. Moments before Doug returned, Nathan acted like he was making one last desperate search of his bag for the pen, and "found" it where it shouldn't have been. Declaring someone must have wrongly packed the bag, he administered the medication. The boy's condition slowly improved, and he was soon transported to a hospital by an ambulance; he eventually had to stay overnight due to the delay in treatment.

Back at the station, their captain demanded to know what had happened. Doug and Nathan both corroborated each other's version of events, and they all agreed that somehow the bag was incorrectly prepared or poorly re-checked. Nathan knew he'd been the one to pack it that morning, but while the captain updated his superiors and the others squared everything away, Nathan used his marine skills to slip unnoticed into the record room and adjust the signature on the paperwork. It was well known that Tom made the odd mistake, so Nathan faked the log to show it was Tom who last checked the med-kit. Nathan practiced his defense all evening because he knew his selected patsy would vociferously dispute the allegations, but he was confident his previous transgressions would tip the balance.

Capt. Mitchell called a meeting first thing the next morning, and he read the riot act to every member of the station. A teenager had almost lost his life because of sloppy preparation. He produced all the paperwork and singled Tom out in front of everyone. He refuted the charge of negligence over and over again, insisting that surely someone must have dealt with the bag since he'd last checked it two days earlier. It wasn't procedure to repack it daily, but most of them made time to double-check all essential kit every day. Of course, Nathan had done just that, but as far as the records showed, Tom was the last man to verify and pack the med-kit. He was given an official reprimand, and Nathan simply kept quiet.

In his downtime, Nathan had become something of a regular at the Through the Looking Glass bar. He'd made friends with a few guys who were both fanatical anti-capitalists; they openly admitted that they felt the best thing that could happen to America was for it to be torn down and rebuilt from scratch. Nathan had spent two weeks preparing a potentially volatile stand-up routine, and two days after he successfully avoided the finger of blame over the EpiPen escapade, he tried out a few of his jokes on some of the regulars. They all concluded it was great, but most normal people would have described the material as outright offensive. His closest associates at the bar lapped it up and repeatedly told him he should perform it at the Impromptu Stand-Up Comedy Night later that week.

Even though he had their unwavering endorsement ringing in his ears, Nathan remained indecisive about whether to get up on stage. The easiest option would have been to not go to the bar that night, but Nathan had never backed down from a challenge and didn't intend to start now. About an hour into the evening, the host opened up the mic for anyone to have a go, and Nathan accepted the invitation. Although he was quite hesitant at times, he delivered the routine he'd previously tested.

His material disgusted a few non-regular drinkers who'd unwittingly picked the bar because of the comedy night, but several of the regulars came up to him afterward and told him they thought he was both funny and right in equal measure. The large-scale acceptance of what he'd said made Nathan feel both welcome and validated. He promised everyone he would have another go in a few weeks.

CHAPTER 6

Emboldened by his positive, outlook-affirming experience in the bar, plus the gratification he felt from recently dispensing his own form of righteous payback, Nathan decided it was time to turn his attention to the people he assumed were responsible for leaving him in Afghanistan. Not only had Nathan wanted to find like-minded people on the dark web, he'd also been seeking out hackers and covert information gatherers who could access the files that he wanted. People could tell them what they wanted to his face, but official reports and military paperwork had to be both accurate and detailed, and it was this intel that Nathan was desperate to obtain. He was conscious not to rely on one person to do everything for him, opting instead for a similar approach to that of fundamentalist terrorists, where each cell was only aware of their own responsibilities and not the entire plan.

One highly skilled blackhat hacker, an unidentified individual who went by the name of "Unstoppable Vengeance", was hired to break into military servers and steal any documents related to the village firefight that were filed by Lt. Lucas Robertson. It took Nathan quite a while to convince his anonymous associate that he was genuine and not a plant, and even more time to set up a system of payment that was untraceable. UV eventually agreed once Nathan offered to pay him $25k, via cryptocurrency and upon delivery, to provide the classified documents he required. It was impossible to tell whether the money was the real draw for UV or simply the challenge of hacking the Department of Defense mainframes. Four days after striking the deal, Nathan received a message containing all of Robertson's documents. With his request fulfilled, he made the payment.

As he sat at his desk, he paused for a moment and looked over at the photos of his daughter. There was a small part of him that genuinely hoped Robertson's reports and briefing papers would actually show he did everything that Nathan could have asked and, in the end, had simply made a tough call. The hateful side of him quickly countered with the thought that whatever actions Robertson had taken, rightly or wrongly, his decisions had still played a part in the loss of his family. He opened the documents one at a time and read them slowly and carefully. At first, there was no information that he didn't already know; after all, he was there and witnessed everything just as Robertson had. The lieutenant praised Nathan for his quick thinking once they had discovered the weapons cache, and also highlighted everything he did to keep his men alive. There was little Nathan could fault or disagree with when it came to the historical account of the battle. That all changed when he got to the backend of the reports.

Contained within the latter pages of the illegally obtained files was a confession that left Nathan stunned. As Robertson detailed the final moments of their clash with the insurgents, his reports admitted—clearly and without any ambiguity—that when he ordered his troops to retreat, he was unsure whether Nathan Profit was actually dead. In fact, his official statement of events confirmed that he knew there was a very good chance that his staff sergeant was still alive, but that Lt. Robertson "assumed" his wounds were so serious that it wasn't worth the risk of delaying the E-Vac or returning a few hours later to rescue him. Nathan had always been given the impression that his comrades had acted as they did because they were certain he was dead. He didn't like it and had it been his call, he would have ensured that the person was actually dead, but at least he could understand the decision. To now read that not only was his commanding officer unsure, but that he felt it very probable that Nathan was actually still alive… he was left speechless. His shock very quickly turned to incendiary rage that someone he trusted so willingly and so implicitly had left him behind, knowing he wasn't dead.

That unequivocal admission changed everything for Nathan when it came to Lieutenant Lucas Robertson. That man had left him for dead and now bore direct responsibility for everything he'd suffered. Had he acted differently, honorably, and made every effort to rescue Nathan, he was certain none of what he'd endured would have happened! He'd lost everything, and now he would ensure that the same happened to Lt. Robertson, so he would also feel the anguish and hopelessness that Nathan had been through.

Wasting little time, he immediately went back onto the dark web and began searching for contacts who, for the right price, would be willing to carry out the tasks that would quench Nathan's thirst for vengeance. On the dark web, you can find anyone willing to do anything… if the money is right. He visited various chat rooms and message boards, some with requests and people searching for services that turned even his stomach, and finally he connected with a small group of people who were vigilante-like, but they didn't restrict their endeavors to those who simply broke the law.

He transferred $100k to them with a specific set of demands. Two of them were to obtain an untraceable vehicle, stolen or otherwise, and follow Robertson and his family wherever they went. The first evening/night they saw the family crossing a quiet street together—and that part was crucial because, under no circumstances, did Nathan want this to be a public spectacle

—the two assailants were to run the family down. If at all possible, he wanted Robertson to be the sole survivor of the hit 'n' run, but that was merely a "bonus" and not a necessity. Nearly a week after he'd paid the group, his wrathful urge to seek "an eye for an eye" was appeased. He was sitting at home when his cell phone rang, and he saw that it was Dwayne.

"Hey, Nath, listen, I got some bad news, man. I just got a call from Captain Anderson… there has been an accident. Lieutenant Robertson was out earlier this evening with his family… they were crossing the road—it's reckoned they were on their way to a restaurant or sumthin'—and they were run down by a speeding car. The police are working on that basis that it was a bunch of junkies who'd stolen the vehicle and gone for a joyride."

Making sure he sounded as surprised as possible, he quickly asked, "Fuck me, Dwayne, are they okay? When can we go and see them? I'll tell you what, let me know which hospital they are at, and I will meet—"

"Hold up, man," interrupted Dwayne. "After all you have been through, I hate to be the one to have to tell you this, but there's no urgency. Nath, they pronounced Lucas dead at the scene from head injuries and internal bleeding. His wife, Marta, and their youngest son, Lee, were both killed as well. They rushed the oldest son to the nearest E.R. department, but according to Anderson and the hospital staff he spoke to, his chances ain't great."

"Is there anything we can do? When one of the guys was in a bad way, we'd usually send some things to lift their spirits when they woke up, but this is a buddy's kid. Is there anything else I can do?" asked Nathan.

"Not really, maybe say a few prayers for him if you're so inclined. Hey, I gotta go… errr, I will let you know if I hear any more news. Listen, do me a favor will you, make sure you speak to someone in the next few days. It doesn't matter to me if it's one of your councilors or even someone at work. You've been through a lot, and something like this has a way of having a sneakily bigger impact than you initially think. Alright?" asked Dwayne.

"I promise," he replied wearily, having no intention of doing so.

They both said their goodbyes and the phone went dead. He may have put on his best concerned and surprised mask for Dwayne, but the reality was that Nathan was overjoyed. The man directly responsible for his predicament had paid the ultimate cost. It seemed like a lot of money last week, but now his online associates had carried out his wishes, it was cheap at twice the price. He poured himself a stiff whiskey to celebrate, and for a short while contemplated whether he should take action to finish off the remaining son. In the end, he decided it wasn't worth the risk or the cost. His only regret was that the driver had killed Robertson in the collision, and that he'd not lived long enough to experience the loss of his family. Nathan slept very well that night and didn't feel any regret whatsoever for his actions.

He did everything that would be expected of him over the weeks that followed. He visited the son in hospital, attended the funeral of Lt. Robertson and his family, and even organized a couple of charity events with other marines to raise money for the son who was still alive. Nathan managed to rope in the fire station as well, and arranged an open day and a charity car wash. People showered him with plaudits for his dedication to helping his dead comrade's son. Both the normal Washington Police Department and the Quantico Military Police worked tirelessly to apprehend the perpetrators, but aside from a seriously burnt out car they recovered ten days after the collision, the authorities turned up nothing. As much as he wanted to proceed to the next phase and investigate the involvement of Captain Justin Anderson, Nathan was more than aware he had to be patient. If Anderson was suddenly the victim of an "accident" so soon after Robertson's untimely demise, someone might start digging.

Whether it was down to luck or focusing too much attention on his military retribution, Nathan had been a good boy at work. There had been no recent call-outs that involved someone who he deemed worthy of his special attention. That was no bad thing because even Nathan accepted he couldn't take action day in and day out. Besides, with the awful state of the country he gave so much to protect, it wouldn't be long before he attended a scene that involved yet another piece of undeserving trash.

That thought process proved to be absolutely correct. The station had experienced an exceptionally quiet day when an urgent mid-evening call-out came through from dispatch. One of the local college football teams was in the middle of a game, and there had been a serious collision that involved several players. The two on-scene ambulances were in the process of dealing with three badly injured players, two of which had head and neck trauma, but they would soon have to leave the game to transport the players to the hospital. With no other ambulance teams available, it fell to Nathan's crew, seeing as he was a fully qualified paramedic, to provide temporary cover until one of the ambulances could return. Just two plays after they arrived, there was another vicious hit that left a senior home team player writhing in agony. Nathan and Clarissa rushed out to assist, and it was obvious to both of them that he'd done serious damage to his shoulder.

They eventually got him to the sideline and the game continued. Nathan immediately observed that there was a noticeable lack of concern or interest in his condition from the rest of the team. Bar the coaches who popped over to check on him, no one else seemed remotely bothered that he was seriously hurt. As he assessed the injury with Clarissa, he metaphorically pinned his ears back to see whether he could ascertain why no-one else was worried about the health of their "star" running back. He picked up what sounded like unhappy grumbling, but he couldn't hear clearly what was being said. Nathan decided to quickly contrive an excuse that he needed to go over to the engine for equipment, so he could walk past the players and get a better idea of what they were saying. On his way there, he heard a snippet of one conversation.

"Dude, with Trey and Michael on their way to the local hospital, and now Geno out with a fucked shoulder, we've lost this game," lamented the first.

"Yeah, well, Geno ain't no star running back, and you know it. He's only the starter 'cause his old man donates a stack of cash to the athletic department. The guy's father virtually funds the team… you reckon he'd be startin' if it weren't for that? Ricardo is twice the player he is, and yet he spends the whole fuckin' game on the bench," bemoaned a second player.

On his way back, Nathan caught part of another conversation.

"I'd like to see them keep Ricardo on the bench now. He earned that starting job during the off-season, then in walks Geno's "pappa" and suddenly his son's given the job or "daddy" will turn off the money tap. Shit, he weren't even here half the time," said a scornful teammate.

"Bit late now though… Ricardo's already lost all the best options he might have had because he ain't played much this year. Bet Geno's ol' man has already been onto various scouts…"

Nathan tried to slow the pace of his assessment and treatment as much as he could without causing any questions from Clarissa. Comments like "Given it on a platter", "Rich man's son gets what he wants", and "Trampled over other more talented players just because he can" were all quietly uttered just out of the injured player's earshot.

Undeserving, self-centered, classless, full of entitlement and without morals, here was yet another prime recipient. Nathan couldn't do much to help Ricardo's prospects, but he could make sure he got a shot to play in the final three games.

"It's possibly a torn rotator cuff, and it's definitely a little out of joint," he stated to Clarissa. "I need to be careful here; I think I can pop it back in, but I need to keep the motion as small as possible."

"Wouldn't it be better to wait and let the hospital do it… at least they can do an M.R.I. on it first?" she queried.

"We could, but the kid will have no chance to play again this year; this way, I might be able to restrict the damage," hinted Nathan.

She thought it over for a few moments, then apprehensively agreed with her colleague. Nathan had one problem if he wanted to teach the kid a lesson. Clarissa was right there with him, and now he'd already gone to get the spare med-kit, he was out of excuses to get her to leave him alone for a few minutes. There was nothing in the engine he could ask for that she couldn't whip out from one of the bags, and this time he had no opportunity to hide something that could be found later. He was also too well-trained to simply damage the shoulder accidentally, and that would likely result in some form of investigation.

With Clarissa in close proximity, it seemed like the pampered, over-privileged, detestable specimen in front of him would avoid any unfortunate accident. As he was about to treat the injury correctly, Nathan noticed that there were just seconds left in the 3rd quarter, at which point the umpire would blow a loud whistle. It would be a shame if it made him jump as he was putting Geno's shoulder back in place! Aiming to time it just right, he adjusted his position, so he could see the clock out the corner of his eye. Nathan placed one hand around Geno's wrist, the other on his shoulder.

"Clarissa, can you please try to hold him steady because I need his movement to be as minimal as possible? Geno, I am sorry to say, this is going to hurt, son. Please try as hard as you can not to move when I pop it back in," Nathan requested.

Normally, he would have tried to use his own weight to reduce any movement by his patient, but that was for people he wanted to help; he didn't want to help Geno and the more he could move, the more chance the procedure would cause harm. With all three of them prepared, Nathan watched the clock as the last ten seconds ticked down.

"Ready… three… two… one…"

The umpire blew his whistle and fireworks unexpectedly went off in the background. The situation turned out better than he could have wished. His quick reactions allowed him to time his fully intended mistake right on the bangs of the fireworks. Nathan fell awkwardly to one side and twisted the shoulder almost as far out of joint the other way. Geno roared in pain, then Nathan recoiled backward and looked over at Clarissa with an expression of absolute horror.

"For God's sake, Nathan, what happened?" she shouted angrily.

With his arm even more limp than before, Geno was clearly in utter agony.

"Fuck, fuck, fuck… I'm so sorry, the fireworks went off and they made me jump. Shit, what have I done?" he said in a panic, his performance worthy of an Oscar nomination.

He "attempted" to pull himself together, but Clarissa had seen enough and took over the situation.

"Nathan, I think you had better go over to the truck. Can you get Peter to call for an ambulance? We probably ought to leave this as it is now, just in case we do any further damage. Actually, get Doug to come over as well, will ya? Seriously, just go and wait somewhere over there," Clarissa partly suggested, partly almost ordered.

Nathan went and stood by the bleachers. It quickly dawned on him that he had probably just made his first major mistake. He hadn't intended to go quite so far, but when the bangs of the fireworks went off, it seemed to instantly provide the perfect cover for his actions; he knew this was the reason he never did anything on the spur of the moment. An instantaneous decision never allowed time to fully evaluate any potential ramifications from that course of action. Now, he had to think quickly to devise a believable and realistic response to the questions that undoubtedly would be asked. Once the others had completed the patient handover to the ambulance team, Clarissa walked over to Nathan for a quiet discussion.

"What in God's name happened there, Nathan? I wasn't entirely happy with your suggested treatment as it was, but now..."

She turned and looked at the game for a minute, then spun around to face him once more.

"You seemed to have everything in hand, then bang... the kid's leaving in an ambulance with his shoulder ligaments in pieces. You know I am going to have to file a report with the captain?" she said almost awkwardly.

"As you should," he replied, seizing the opportunity to take control of the situation. "I have no excuses. I am still completely happy with what we intended to do, and I have no excuse over what happened. The sudden bangs from the fireworks just freaked me out. It is the first time I have been around fireworks since I got back. You know, I have seen P.T.S.D. jump up, literally out of nowhere, on other ex-marines... I never thought I would be one of them," he confessed with fake sincerity.

"I know we all make mistakes, but damn, Nathan, you really messed up his shoulder. I suspect the captain will want you to be evaluated again, if only to be on the safe side…"

"And I'll agree to it as well, you can be sure of that," he butted in.

"After what you went through, maybe this shouldn't be a complete surprise. I am pretty sure Capt. Mitchell and Lt. Spencer wouldn't put you anywhere with loud bangs and explosions by choice. It did come out of nowhere, and even I flinched a bit. Listen, let's just get back to the station. I suppose it could happen to the best of us… if something goes bang like that at just the right second."

"I appreciate the support. Whatever the captain decides, he will get no dispute from me. It shouldn't have happened, Clarissa. I can't ignore that, no matter what he does or doesn't decide. All I can do is make sure that it doesn't happen again," he assured her.

His final comment was about the only truthful thing he said to her. Nathan's eagerness to make use of the available, somewhat useful circumstances, rather than wait for the situation to be perfectly right for him to act, had very nearly exposed him. How prophetic she had been when she said we all make mistakes, but now he had no room for error; one mistake could be explained away, another would likely see him placed under increased scrutiny.

The two of them walked back to the engine together, and the whole team left once the game was over. Captain Mitchell had gone home by the time they got back to the station, so Clarissa had to wait until the next morning to file her report. The overnight delay gave Nathan extra time to solidify his response, and he worked into the early hours to make sure he had every possible response and reaction covered. Regardless of what she had said, he knew he had raised some suspicion within Clarissa, and now he had to be extra cautious when she was around.

CHAPTER 7

The next morning went very much as Nathan had expected it to. Within a few minutes of his arrival at the station, Captain Mitchell called Clarissa, Lt. Spencer, and Nathan into his office. Clarissa had prepared her report overnight and already handed it to her senior officer. Rather than discuss its contents with the trio on the other side of his desk, his first course of action was to ask Nathan what had happened the night before. Nathan had prepared for every eventuality he could think of, including this one, but was still a little surprised that the station chief had taken that approach to simply ask him about it first. He guessed it was possibly an attempt to trip Nathan up, an opportunity where the probationary member of his team might contradict his colleague's statement or inadvertently lie as he tried to cover his own ass. If that was the case, they had grossly misjudged him because there was no chance that Nathan would make such an unforced error.

"I have no excuse to offer, Captain," he began confidently. "I diagnosed a potential torn rotator cuff, a minor one as far as I could tell, and a disjointed shoulder. I knew the longer it remained out of place, the higher the risk that the tear could worsen. Therefore, I suggested to Clarissa that the increased risk could be reduced if I popped the shoulder back into…"

"Surely, if you thought it was torn, you should have waited for the ambulance to return and take him to hospital where an M.R.I. could be done?" interrupted Mitchell.

"Clarissa did indeed make that suggestion, sir," he stated. He wanted to give her credit, so he could appear humble in his defense. "I did consider that approach, but I also understood it was in my patient's best interest to limit the severity of the injury as much as possible, in the hope he could return to playing sooner than he could if the tear worsened."

Nathan paused…

"I see the logic, although I'm not sure that I agree with the decision. However, Clarissa has confirmed that she did support the suggestion at the time," Mitchell confirmed.

"I asked Clarissa to help secure the patient, and prepared to softly and gently manipulate the shoulder back into place. I didn't want to use force to get it back in, more try to see if I could ease it into the socket. If the minor, low intensity approach had failed, it was my intention to revert to Clarissa's recommendation to strap it up and allow the hospital to administer treatment. As I made the first tentative movement, a batch of fireworks went off that startled me, in the extreme, and instead of a minor manipulation, the instantaneous movement of my body twisted the shoulder too far the other way. Sir, I am horrified that my uncontrolled reaction to the loud explosions has resulted in my harming a patient, and I accept any and all recommendations you intend to make. I know that I have achieved a lot since my return from Afghanistan, but it is obvious that I still have some things to work through. If my potential P.T.S.D. is an issue, I am prepared to do what is necessary to avoid a repeat."

Nathan had rehearsed the calculated and very specific description of events several times. He had to ensure it perfectly matched Clarissa's report to head off any further questions surrounding what actually happened. He couldn't change what he'd done or the actions that he now knew were reckless, but he at least had some sway over damage control.

"I admire your honesty, Nathan. This is indeed a serious issue, but it's not like you intentionally harmed the patient. I understand your course of action and accept the extenuating circumstances that played a large part in what transpired yesterday evening. Both myself and the area commander have spoken to the boy's father this morning, and while initially he wanted to take the matter further and have you suspended pending an investigation, he has since withdrawn that request. Both his own father and his grandfather served in the armed forces, and once I explained your unique background, he became far more accommodating. If you willingly agree to increase your counseling appointments, and any additional therapies for conditions such as P.T.S.D., he is willing to let the matter rest. You will receive an official reprimand, and a caution will go on your service record. As a probationer, that would normally be the end of your career, but again, we are aware of the value you bring to the service and mindful of your past, so a one-off exception will be made. If anything like this happens again, there will be no such leniency."

The last few words came as a relief to Nathan. He was confident he could talk his way out of any serious repercussions, but it wasn't a certainty.

"Unless Clarissa or Lt. Spencer has anything to add, that is the end of the matter?" finished Capt. Mitchell.

They both confirmed their agreement with his decision, and the chief declared the meeting over. He wasn't sure if he imagined it, but Nathan swore Clarissa was giving him just a little extra attention when he spoke. She may not have said it and her report may not have declared it, but it was the final proof he needed that his concern about her beginning to sense something might be going on was correct.

To lift the glare of suspicion from his colleague and to validate the faith shown by his station commander, Nathan once again reverted to making sure everything he did was totally by the book. He allowed the perfectionist marine to guide his every action and ensure there were no genuine mistakes and no intentional ones. In an effort to erase the negativity of that night, Nathan thought it would help to lean more on the caring father/understanding ex-husband facets of his purpose-built public persona. He managed to persuade Lisa to make their meetings a little more regular, and he went out of his way to get some photos of Charlotte on his phone that he could show the rest of his workmates. Impressed by his dedication, Lisa even brought Charlotte to the station a couple of times to see how he was doing. He put on his best facade and pretended to be absolutely thrilled she was taking an interest in her ex-husband's new career, and allowing Charlotte a brief look into "what mommy's friend does for a job." He showed his colleagues and his boss how everything was fine between them, and how happy he was for her. It took everything he had to behave in such a false way when he actually felt unbridled hostility and continued rage that she had also abandoned him.

In his downtime when he was alone at home, Nathan had started to come to the conclusion that he needed to slightly modify his approach. He still had nothing but disgust for the societal vermin he encountered that infested many parts of the American public, but they would always be there, regardless of how many low-life scumbags he retaliated against. Instead, he mused, maybe it was time to turn his attention back to one specific part of the community… the section that bore all the responsibility for the situation that was forced upon him. It was time to pause his crusade on the human garbage that surrounded him and redouble his efforts to savagely strike back at the military that thought so little of his life.

His crusade gained an unexpected bonus in the week that followed, something that Nathan's ever-worsening warped mind viewed as proof from a higher power, not necessarily God but from the universe in general, that his campaign had received cosmic approval.

The dispatch headquarters had issued a large-scale call-out for ambulances and paramedic-supported fire crews to attend the scene of a shoot-out between police and members of a local gang in one of the district's rougher suburbs. By the time Nathan's team arrived, the two ambulance crews on-scene had begun a triage assessment of the victims. The incident involved two police cars and four officers, plus three gang-related 4x4s and five offenders. The E.M.T. responders had pronounced two criminals dead already. One medic focused their attention on a third who was in critical condition, and the remaining two gang members with significant but non-fatal wounds received attention from the other medic in that team. Across the street, the other ambulance crew had declared one officer dead, while the two medics worked on the three remaining officers. The first had a heavily bleeding leg wound, the second had taken bullets in both the arm and the shoulder, and the third was in critical condition with a stomach wound.

Part of Nathan really wanted to treat the gang members, but would the allure of inflicting harm in the name of justice be too strong? In addition, might a fatality to a gangland patient once again be too obvious? Even if it was unintentional and the natural course of things, might he still get the blame for it? Two of the medics at the scene were rookies, so the senior E.M.T. yelled at Nathan to take over treatment of the stomach wound officer, so he could switch his focus to aiding the less experienced responders. The man had been willing to lay down his life to stop the waste of oxygen on the other side of the street, so Nathan took pride in his opportunity to help someone truly deserving of care. That opinion changed in a heartbeat when the E.M.T. filling him in on the specific details explained that the cop had previously served as a marine in Afghanistan.

He knew that everyone would expect him to do absolutely everything he could to save a fellow marine… why wouldn't he? Here was a man that had been through similar experiences, that had already put his life on the line for his country on active service, and now done so again as a law enforcement officer. No matter how strongly Nathan told himself that this was too high a profile situation to extract retribution, his hatred of the Marine Corps overwhelmed his rational mind that unquestionably knew this wasn't the time nor the place. He looked around specifically for Clarissa, and she was involved in treating the gang members on the other side of the road. Everyone else was frantically working on other patients, all of which were fairly well spread out. He was safely alone with the ex-soldier.

"Don't worry, Officer Russell, you're going to be just fine. You got a fellow ex-marine here, one who also served in Afghanistan, looking after you. You don't need me to tell you that you took a nasty hit here, but everything is going to be alright," he assured the fallen policeman.

He felt a perverse sense of enjoyment from constantly telling his victim that it would all be okay, when he knew full well exactly what he was about to do. Nathan guessed the former military man would have at least some medical knowledge, so he had to be precise with his actions. At first, he put pressure exactly where it was needed with one hand and used the other to rummage in his med-kit. Slowly, inch by inch, he adjusted the pressure of his hand on the wound. The cop was already quite vague and semi-conscious, so Nathan felt confident he wouldn't be shouting out to anyone. He pressed a little harder on the right spot and instead of helping to stop the blood flow, he actually began pushing it out. As the seconds passed, the officer's chances of survival slipped away, and when he was sure it was irreversible, he screamed out for assistance from other medics.

"Help, someone, get over here! I need another set of hands or we're gonna lose him," he shouted frantically.

He wasn't sure if he was happy or should be concerned when it was Clarissa that appeared from the far side of the car that propped up the officer.

"Clarissa, you gotta help me. I've done all I can, but I can't stop the bleeding. Can you put pressure here while I see if I can stem the flow?" he begged.

His colleague reacted swiftly and did everything she could to help him save the officer's life. She could see he'd lost a lot of blood, and yet remained blissfully unaware of quite how much Nathan had let pour out. Two more ambulance teams turned up, and the first hurried over to the officer with the stomach wound. They knew he had to be rushed to hospital if he was to have any chance of survival, and so they immediately took over, moved him to a stretcher and took him off to the nearest E.R. department.

The fire crew stayed at the scene for another forty minutes, and when there were enough ambulance teams on site, they returned to the station. En-route, they received a radio message from Captain Mitchell, who informed them that Officer Russell had died on his way to the hospital. The head officer of the Washington P.D. had asked him to pass on the department's immense gratitude for everything that Nathan had tried to do in his attempt to save Officer Russell's life.

Nathan spotted a particularly cynical opportunity ahead of him. To gain sympathy from the rest of the team, he put on a fake act of depression and upset over the loss of a fellow soldier. He couldn't save one of his brothers and was devastated about it. Mitchell even gave him two days compassionate leave to allow him time to reflect and come to terms with what happened. Secretly, he felt exactly the opposite. He had destroyed the lives of another ex-serviceman's family, and he was proud of what he'd done. Nathan even raised a couple of toasts that night—in honor that ex-marine Russell would rot in hell.

He felt reinvigorated, and allowed his mind to contemplate the possibility of unleashing his wrath on the other surviving members of his unit. No one had ever suspected any premeditated foul play in the death of Lucas Robertson, so now with a decent amount of time having passed, he debated numerous ways that he could ruin the lives of the three surviving marines. He began to form the basis of an elaborate scheme that would involve a set of unconnected dark web contacts who would each be responsible for one unrelated part of the operation.

He knew that one of the marines came from a highly respected, well-off military family, so he could arrange for someone to break into his house with the intention of stealing valuable family heirlooms. The thieves could "inadvertently" alert the occupants and this would result in a near fatal, or hopefully, fatal shooting. Another of his intended victims was well known for his fast car and driving recklessly on the back road route to his home; Nathan felt it would be a shame if a mechanical fault resulted in a serious, life-ending crash! Lastly, an unexpected moment of inspiration watching a film gave him the idea to secretly poison the family of the third marine via an unseen injection into an item of shopping. He thought it would be a shame that the shop owner would face serious questions, but that was acceptable collateral damage.

As much as he enjoyed the time that he'd spent plotting and scheming, Nathan always knew he couldn't realistically carry out any of his suggestions… no matter how much he ached to do so. If one or two senior officers from the same brigade were to pass away through random acts of violence or accidents, it was doubtful anyone would consider that a particularly dubious event. However, if Lt. Robertson and then three of the five remaining marines from a particular mission suddenly died, there was no way that wouldn't raise red flags. He desperately wanted to make those three grunts pay for their lack of courage and conviction, for breaking the Marine Oath and leaving fellow soldiers behind; not only the dead bodies, but someone still breathing. Part of him wanted to say, "Screw it!" and do it anyway, damn the consequences, but he had so much more that he wanted to do… so much that he needed to do!

If he was going to go after the three of them, it would need to be over years, not months or weeks. For now, the lower ranks, the sniveling brown nosers who said nothing when their officer turned tail and ran, would get a reprieve. Having entertained himself for a couple of evenings, he settled down in front of his laptop and logged on to the dark web. If he couldn't go after the cannon fodder, he would have to turn his attention to the people who made the decisions.

"Now, let's see what Captain Justin Anderson had to say in response to the report filed by that cowardly bastard Robertson…"

CHAPTER 8

The gratification and pleasure that Nathan felt following his fatal interaction with Officer Russell lasted for several days. He still couldn't believe that life had presented him with such a perfect opportunity to strike back at an ex-member of the armed forces. He had almost exposed his real intentions a couple of times, and yet just when he needed it, the strangeness of fate and destiny reared up to put him in exactly the right place at the right time. It was a bonus to be able to send Officer Russell on his way, but it wasn't something he wanted to do often. His role as a first responder was to allow him to distribute his own form of justice on the dregs of society that had long since ruined the country he once loved. It was never supposed to become blurred with his personal crusade against the military.

He put his two days of compassionate leave to good use. Having finally decided that any action against the lower ranks of his previous unit would be far too suspicious, he opted instead to focus the remainder of his time on trying to uncover exactly what Captain Anderson knew and what orders he gave following Nathan's capture. As before, he carefully trawled the nefarious recesses of the dark web to enlist the help of another hacker who would be willing to obtain the information he required. He wanted someone totally unconnected with the person who secured the reports from Lt. Robertson, and though a few potential options surfaced, there wasn't anyone he felt he could trust.

Before he knew it, his two days were over, and it was time for him to return to work. He wanted to milk his colleagues' sympathy for every last ounce of compassion that he could obtain from the situation. He played the "Lost in thought/Looking distant" card a few times, the others in his crew telling him they understood how hard the death of Officer Russell must have been for him. The one he wanted to sucker in the most was Clarissa; he needed to make sure that he banished as much of her mistrust as feasibly possible.

During the second morning, he paused in the station mess room after the other guys had left, knowing full well that she would walk in a few minutes later to fill her water bottle. He gazed out of the window, failing to acknowledge her when she strolled in, then as she stood at the sink, he began to cry. It surprised him how hard it was to fake tears; those pathetic Hollywood actors and the disgusting examples that plagued reality shows seemed to turn on the water works at will.

"You alright, Nathan?" she inquired with genuine concern.

"Yeah, sorry… Officer Russell just popped into my head. That poor kid. He managed two tours with the marines, once in Iraq and once in Afghanistan. He survives all that, and then he gets taken out by a bunch of gang-bangers in Washington. Where is the fairness in that?"

He may have found the tears tough to fake, but his words literally dripped with sincerity and sadness. He had to manufacture that sort of thing so often since his captivity that it was now second nature.

"Oh, Nath, you did all you could. I was there, remember? I know you beat yourself up over what happened to that football player, and that was a tough break, but there is no way you can blame any of this on yourself. That officer had suffered a serious gunshot wound, and I doubt he would have lived as long as he did, had it not been for you," she assured him.

He looked over at her with tear-filled eyes. "Thanks, Clarissa. It means a lot. Give me a moment and I'll be okay."

She smiled back at him and wandered out the room, pausing for just a few seconds to rest a comforting hand on his shoulder. Had there been a mirror on the far wall instead of a window, she would have seen a wicked, vicious smile creep across his face. Having given himself enough time to "clear his head", he strolled out and joined the rest of the crew in the daily briefing.

In truth, he could have carried on the charade for weeks, but he didn't want to overplay his hand. Nathan felt he had achieved what he set out to do, and being a tough ex-marine who'd been to hell and back, he knew there was an expiration date on his emotional distress. When he felt he had played the distraught brother-in-arms long enough, Nathan decided to switch from playing on their sympathy to pursuing their admiration for his attempts to "come to terms" with his inability to save Officer Russell. It was all completely calculated, but it seemed to work and that was all that mattered.

He may have wanted to focus on trying to administer his own form of malevolent reprisal against the unworthy in his day job, but it seemed fate once again had other ideas. A few days after he returned to work, Mitchell called a meeting that involved everyone in the station; he even called in those who were on leave. Such a large-scale meeting was an unusual occurrence, and it often signaled either a major announcement involving the station itself or that the crew were due to be assigned to a special fixture involving the public. On this occasion, it was the latter.

Captain Mitchell spent an hour informing everyone that senior officials had selected the station as one of four to provide both fire and paramedic cover at a huge military event that was scheduled to take place over the upcoming weekend. It would include air dogfights, parachute displays and all manner of other military pageantry. Little more than five minutes of the briefing session had elapsed, and Nathan had already decided he wanted nothing to do with it. There were far too many members of the public that were in need of his unique treatment, a day at a military regatta would consume valuable time that he felt would be better spent elsewhere. Short of taking a sick-day, which would seem odd for an ex-serviceman who apparently still adored his fellow pals in the armed forces, it quickly became obvious there was little chance he would be able to avoid it. The captain mentioned numerous times that one of the deciding factors was the station's ex-marine celebrity, who the military top brass organizing the event had specifically asked for.

Fuckin' great, he thought to himself. This will be about as enjoyable as an afternoon with Khalid and Samandy.

Nathan didn't really hear very much from the rest of the meeting. He gave the impression he was listening, but his attention was miles away as he tried to scheme some way of getting out of it. By the time his captain had finished, he was well aware there was no chance of that.

I could just injure myself, he thought.

That would work to get him out of the weekend's "festivities" but would likely see him off work for a week, maybe longer, as it would need to be more than a sore ankle or wrist. By the end of the next day, like it or not, Nathan had accepted the inevitable and resigned himself to being at the show. It actually got worse because a second diktat came down from head office that confirmed the people running the event wanted Nathan there on both days; bar the four station captains, he was the only other responder given the "privilege" of being there the whole weekend.

The organizers requested that the four engine crews, along with their colleagues in the ambulance service, be onsite at 7a.m., two hours before the gates opened to the public. Nathan never had an issue with getting up early, but he was noticeably a little pricklier at the station before they left. He knew he had to rein that in quickly because everyone assumed that Nathan would see it as a huge honor to be at the show. There were many words he could think of that would sum up how he felt... honored wasn't one of them.

Once in position at the airfield, the team set up their hospitality tent next to the engine, and prepared for the oncoming tide of military enthusiasts, plane spotters, and all other manner of spectators. Despite having a fully qualified paramedic, the fire crew's responsibility was primarily to deal with the minor injuries, which would then free up the ambulance teams to treat the more serious conditions and transport them to hospital if necessary. The crew hadn't been on duty for more than twenty minutes when the first casualty came through their tent flaps. In fact, Nathan's first cup of coffee had barely dropped in temperature before he was called into action to treat a child who'd twisted their ankle.

"It's gonna be one of those days," he muttered to himself out of earshot.

He was dead right about that. Between that first hobbling child and the time the marshals closed the gates at 6p.m., some twenty thousand people attended the first day of the show. Nathan was so busy that he had little chance to watch any of the displays or visit anything around the airfield. It actually worked in his favor because there were a few times when the organizers wanted to publicly recognize Nathan Profit for overcoming adversity, but he was "regretfully busy" each time. Throughout the day, he treated numerous small-time, hardly serious injuries and accidents. There were twisted joints, bruised heads from people looking up and not where they were going, a few broken bones that he provisionally helped with before the ambulance teams arrived, some alcohol-related injuries, a couple of fits, and even two people who had simply passed out. Nathan carried out his duties conscientiously and did it all with a smile. Inside, he would have loved to have climbed into the engine and driven it through the middle of the whole damn event!

He didn't get home until nearly 9p.m., and his mood was foul. Prior to his nightmare in Afghanistan, he would have adored the weekend, speaking to all the kids, encouraging the teenagers to consider a role in the military, and taking time to swap stories with retired veterans. He had to strongly resist the urge to get totally wasted on whiskey because it wouldn't help anything for him to arrive the next day stinking of booze. After a microwave dinner, he spent over an hour beating the living daylights out of the new punching bag he'd hung in the garage to assist with his angry outbursts.

"And I get to do it all again tomorrow," he sarcastically mused as he climbed into bed. "Aren't I the fuckin' lucky one..."

Like his own miserable Groundhog Day, Nathan had to repeat the same routine the next morning. He got up early, just as grumpy, made his way to the station and was back again at the airfield for 7a.m.

"Would anyone mind if I drop out of helping set up, so I can go take a look around?" he asked the others.

"Go for it, Nathan," agreed Clarissa. "You already did your bit yesterday, so we'll do the heavy lifting this morning."

There wasn't anything he really wanted to go look at, it was just a chance to have some private time away from the rest of his team. He found a quiet corner and enjoyed a cup of coffee in peace. He could have stayed there all day, or better still, have just snuck out and gone home, but that wasn't an option. Minutes before the marshals opened the gates, he was back at the tent. Whether it was down to a different class of attendee or just pure luck, the second day was substantially quieter. Nathan noticed it early on, and while there were still plenty of "accident-prone cretins", there was nothing like the constant flow of patients that the emergency services had dealt with during the previous day. Around 1p.m., Mitchell told Nathan that he could take a few hours to go and chat with others from the armed forces. He would happily have found an excuse to avoid that opportunity, but with a real lull in incidents and Nathan being on his second day, there was no excuse he could employ.

He left his colleagues in their tent by the truck, and took a stroll among the different concession booths, information kiosks and the various stands devoted to all aspects of the military. There were a couple connected to the marines, and Nathan would have given anything to be able to open fire on them with his old M27. The previous day, there was an impressive parachute display from an airborne marine unit; well, everyone else thought it was superb, Nathan would have happily used a sniper's rifle to pick them off one at a time as they floated through the air. As a first responder, he was in possession of an AAA pass—Access All Areas—and he made use of it to go behind the scenes and talk to the unit involved. As he watched them prepare their equipment, thoughts of intentionally sabotaging one of the parachutes filled his mind.

For what seemed like an age but in reality was merely seconds, Nathan imagined how he'd feel to watch a helpless marine rapidly fall to the ground due to his actions. The horror from the crowd and that satisfying moment when his body would smash into the floor with a dense thud, the impact causing untold physical damage if it was a literal free-fall. He gave it genuine consideration, but his noted appearance behind the scenes would undoubtedly find him in the investigation crosshairs. He felt that uncontrollable urge to act, that need to use the opportunity to inflict maximum harm on a member of the Marine Corps, and absolutely every ounce of control had to be used to resist his desire. Nathan couldn't see it, but he was now displaying multiple signs of being a sociopath or possibly even a psychopath, but in his eyes, his behavior was normal and justified. While he was talking to the parachute team, Nathan spotted that his conversation had distracted one of them to the extent that they had packed their chute incorrectly. Any normal person would have pointed it out straight away; instead, Nathan went out of his way to talk to that marine and make sure he didn't realize his mistake. Not wanting to infringe on their normal preparation routine, Nathan wished them well and left the hangar.

He had to contain his excitement for the next hour or so. For starters, someone could pick up on the error during a double check—it was a fairly obvious mistake—but he also couldn't give any indication he was aware that disaster was near. He returned to the tent and resumed his duties for around forty-five minutes, then asked Mitchell if he could be excused, so he could watch the parachute display that he hadn't seen properly the previous day. The captain agreed to his request, and Nathan made his way through the crowds. Thanks to his AAA pass, he was allowed through the cordon to the very front. He wanted to enjoy the spectacle in all its gruesome glory.

Everything went according to plan at the start; the plane soared to the right altitude and the skydivers leapt out exactly as expected. They performed their acrobatic maneuvers with smoke pouring from their feet, and right on cue, they began deploying their chutes. It took everyone, from those in the crowd to the announcer over the PA, less than ten seconds to see that one of the eight-man team was in real trouble. His chute didn't open properly, and it looked to Nathan like he was possibly wrapped in one or two of his suspension lines. Even from the ground, it was easy to see and feel the panic from the other skydivers. Two marines tried to adjust their trajectory to get closer to him, but due to the rapid pace of his descent, he quickly fell below them. The marine in trouble appeared to make a last-ditch effort, and with seconds to spare, his emergency chute opened with just enough time to somewhat slow his descent. Despite that, the attending crowd could do nothing but watch aghast, with their hands over their mouths, as he plummeted into the ground.

Being a first responder and a paramedic, Nathan leapt up from his seated position on the ground and sprinted over to the badly hurt marine. He was the first medic on the scene and swiftly jumped into action.

"Everyone, give him space, give him space," roared Nathan before asking, "Anyone else here with paramedic training?"

Everyone answered in the negative and Nathan was now the only responder there, probably for the next one to two minutes until the ambulance medics arrived; he could already hear the sirens in the background. The marine was lying flat on his back with blood running from his mouth. Nathan could tell he was still breathing, but he was in critical condition. The impact had caused multiple injuries, including broken bones protruding from both legs and likely smashed ankles, one bone sticking out of his left upper arm, one shoulder massively out of joint and a smashed jawbone. It was almost impossible that he hadn't also suffered broken vertebrae in his back and neck. Other responders were soon on the scene, and Nathan worked diligently with them to stabilize the marine. At this point, the rest of the parachute team were standing around them; how Nathan would have loved to have added to his injuries, but there were too many witnesses. By a twist of fate, Nathan was responsible for securely holding his heavily strapped head and neck when they moved him onto the backboard. Doing everything right and by the book, Nathan was able to covertly ease his fingers under the marine's neck, and though it appeared he was acting correctly, he pushed his fingers up against the lower neck. He felt things move as he did and knew if the marine wasn't paralyzed already, assuming he even lived, then he very likely was now thanks to Nathan's actions.

Once again feigning emotional distress, the blood covered Nathan returned to his crew at the engine. Everyone praised him for reacting so quickly and possibly even saving the marine's life by helping to stabilize him in those crucial first minutes. About an hour before the end of the weekend, the organizers called Nathan up on stage, and he was given a rousing round of applause by the crowd that was left. With things so quiet and after such a disastrous accident, there was little he could do to avoid it. He shyly thanked everyone, gave them a wave and smiled falsely as he left the stage. With the gates closed and the public on their way home, the team packed everything up. They all asked Nathan if he wanted to join them for a drink, but he graciously declined; he was too upset after what had happened and wanted to head home, probably to see if he could speak to his councilor. Everyone expressed their admiration, both for his actions and his honesty.

Later that night, Mitchell phoned to give Nathan an update on the marine. He was still alive, albeit in critical condition, and the E.R. department confirmed his quick thinking did indeed save his life… but he had sustained serious damage to his neck and would likely be paralyzed from the neck down. Sounding upset yet pleased that the marine's chances of survival were somewhat positive, he thanked his commanding officer for the update. Lying in bed that night, a grin spread wide across his face.

"That couldn't have worked out better if I had planned it," he told himself out loud.

He rolled over in bed and let the images of the day fill his mind as he drifted off into his usual, hate-filled dreamland.

CHAPTER 9

Right from the start of the working week, Nathan was eagerly anticipating his regular visit to the Looking Glass tavern. He had performed several routines at the Thursday comedy night, and the once hesitant, unsure comic had now become someone who relished the spotlight. Nathan had started working on new material almost immediately after he'd finished the previous show, and having now honed it and reworked it numerous times, he was ready to unleash his latest routine. With boundaries of taste and decency considered a loose concept by the regulars at the bar, Nathan had long since past the point where he was careful about the jokes he told. It didn't matter whether it was anti-American, sexist, racist, anti-religious or even homophobic gags, nothing was considered sacred.

The days leading up to the latest comedy evening were quieter than usual. There wasn't any particular reason for this; in the life of a first responder, there would always be weeks that felt non-stop and others where it was actually possible to experience boredom. Having extra time on his hands was both a blessing and a curse to Nathan during comedy week. It allowed him an unexpected opportunity to come up with additional jokes, but it also made the week feel longer than usual.

It was during those weeks when Nathan had to be extra careful about how he went about his business. He neither hated nor cared a great deal for his colleagues at the fire station; in fact, he didn't feel much for them at all. None of his crewmates were bad people and none of them were responsible for anything that he'd experienced in recent years, but he simply didn't consider them important to his life or his mission. During quiet periods like this, it was easy for Nathan to let various frustrations boil over and allow his perfect team member mask to slip and show a glimpse of the real Nathan.

A couple of times Tom left the station kitchen in a mess, and that lack of consideration was unacceptable in a busy week, let alone a quiet one. When that happened, Nathan visualized the image of him repeatedly smashing Tom's head against the draining board to remind him of his lack of respect for the rest of the team. He would have loved to have done it for real but had to settle instead for imagining it. Even the usually conscientious Clarissa left the shower area untidy due to rushing out for a family dinner. Disgusted by the messy state that greeted him, Nathan could once again envision himself cracking her head on the white tiles as he repeated how disgraceful her untidiness had been. When those incidents arose, Nathan simply had to resort to the tried-and-tested method of counting to ten or repeating his favorite jokes from the upcoming routine in an attempt to remain calm and placid.

Their call-outs that week had been relatively mundane or rather straightforward for the most part. There were two house fires; one caused by someone leaving a deep fat fryer unattended—an act of abject stupidity, thought Nathan. While the other was down to a cat knocking over a candle from the sideboard that it shouldn't have been on in the first place. Much to the whole station's annoyance, not just Nathan, they were called out the same day to rescue a cat from a tree. It was in the next street over and Nathan swore if it was the same cat that caused the fire, he'd come back that night and skin the bastard—it wasn't.

Possibly the strangest incident they attended that week was a call-out where they had to rescue a parrot that was stuck on a neighbor's roof. Barely able to contain their laughter, Clarissa and Doug nominated Nathan to climb the ladder to free the somewhat rare bird. When he finally reached it, the parrot unleashed a volley of profanity that would make a sailor blush, which caused further hysterics from the others on the ground.

The unusually quiet week would end up having a more serious impact on Nathan's relationship with his colleagues than he could ever have imagined. Unbeknown to Nathan, the Looking Glass bar had started to publicize their Impromptu Stand-Up Comedy Night with an advertising board outside that featured the names of the regular comics and sometimes a photograph. The owner had asked everyone's permission to do so a few weeks earlier, but Nathan was in the middle of celebrating another well-received show with his questionable associates when he was asked, and simply agreed without fully comprehending the owner's intentions. Wednesday had been another low-incident day, so Tom had taken his break later than usual and popped across town to collect a special present for his wife from a store on the same street that housed the bar. As he strolled along the sidewalk, Tom saw the two-sided advertising board, and there on the poster for the show the next evening was a photo of Nathan with his stage name—The Unforgettable Marine. At first, he thought it must have been a mistake, but the photo was clearly Nathan and the fact his comedic handle contained the word "marine" left little room for doubt.

When he got back to the station, while Nathan was busy checking equipment in the truck, Tom told everyone about the tavern's comedy night and their colleague's secret double life as a stand-up comic. He stunned everyone when he told them the news, even Capt. Mitchell, and there was quite a discussion to work out why he hadn't told any of his work friends about the shows. Clarissa wondered if he might be shy getting up on stage in front of people he knew, whereas Doug offered the thought that maybe Nathan simply wanted to keep his work and social life separate. He'd actually hit the nail on the head, but failed to guess the exact reason why he was right. It was Tom who first suggested that they should all go along to the show and support Nathan the next evening. Their station was only on standby between the hours of 9p.m. and 6a.m., so Tom proposed that they all went after they had finished work. Lt. Spencer was the first one to raise a concern about the team gate-crashing Nathan's show without warning, but they would be off-duty, so he couldn't order them not to attend. Doug, Tom, Peter, and Clarissa slept on it overnight, and all agreed the next morning that they would attend later that evening.

Nathan was blissfully unaware of his colleagues' good intentions and would have likely gone stratospheric had he known. They dropped a couple of very subtle hints, but being totally clueless about the advertising board outside the bar, Nathan never twigged. As the end of their shift grew closer, Clarissa started to have second thoughts. The idea that maybe Nathan didn't tell them because he didn't want to perform in front of friends and family made her feel a little uncomfortable, and she suggested that maybe they should leave Nathan to it. The other three were adamant that they wanted to see his show and prove to Nathan that his colleagues were 100% behind him. Begrudgingly, she eventually agreed to go with them.

Nathan may have left the Marine Corps, but the regimented military man was still very much the core of his being. He followed the same habitual sequence every time he was due to take the stage at the Glass. Due to his job, it was always possible he would have to cancel at the last minute due to a call-out, and the owner and announcer were very much aware of that. Assuming that didn't happen, Nathan always left five minutes early on the night he was due to perform. His pre-performance ritual was to drive straight home, give his material a read through, have a meal, read it through all again, then grab a cab and head to the bar. He went through everything in that order prior to leaving and arrived at the Glass in high spirits, absolutely raring to go and excited to see the reaction to his latest jokes.

As usual, he chose a table near the stage, ordered a couple of beers, and waited for the announcer to call him to the mic. Feeling so comfortable in the tavern, Nathan unusually sat with his back to the audience and the rest of the bar. Like many people in the armed forces, he would usually sit facing into the room with his back to a wall; he knew countless people who did the exact same thing because being always alert was something ingrained in their psyche. Had he taken a seat, like normal, that faced the door and the open room, he would have seen his four colleagues enter the bar at around 10p.m. However, sitting at the front with his back to the room, he never noticed them enter. They quickly realized he hadn't seen them come in, and wanting to surprise him as much as possible, the quartet took a table in the back corner that was dimly lit. Even when Nathan went to the bar for another beer, their discrete position meant it was unlikely he would notice them unless he knew to look directly at the table.

The fortnightly comedy evening was much the same each time. A week before the show, the bar would reach out to the regulars and see who wanted to book a slot. They were always allocated four, sometimes five, of the eight possible openings; the others would be saved for the actual night to be dished out to spur-of-the-moment entries. If no-one accepted the offer, they gave the regulars longer on stage. Nathan was the penultimate comic that evening, and he patiently waited for his turn. After the first regular comic, whose act was fairly run-of-the-mill bawdiness, two customers bravely took to the stage, but they were shot down quickly because the regulars didn't appreciate their "woke" style of humor.

That was the moment Clarissa first started to sense something wasn't right. She wasn't a prude, far from it, there were some rather crass, insensitive comedians who she utterly adored.

However, the negative reaction to two comics using mainstream, quite acceptable jokes left her perturbed. When the second regular comedian took to the stage with an act that contained countless, bile-filled jokes about women and foreigners, her concern increased. By this point, even the three guys were starting to voice their discomfort about the material that was being widely applauded around the room.

Had Nathan known who was in attendance, he would never have stepped on the stage. His friends from the station all agreed they would be quiet when he took over the mic, and only make their presence known once he'd finished his act. Their plan was to cheer loudly from the back, assuming he hadn't spotted them, then walk down to the front clapping and whooping when he'd finished. The announcer came to the stage, gave Nathan a huge build up, then invited him to take over. There was a massive cheer from all around the room, and it was clear to his colleagues that he was a popular performer. If that hadn't concerned the four of them enough, the next twenty-five minutes certainly did. Anyone who has been on a live stage knows that the crowd is often obscured from view by the brightness of the spotlights and the darkness beyond the edge of the stage. When Nathan Profit took the mic from its stand to begin his performance, the only people he could see were those in the front row; beyond that, he couldn't see anything. He couldn't see his colleagues, nor the look of apprehension on their faces as he began. Nathan tore through a set of quick-fire jokes that were about as offensive as they could possibly be; some might argue they bordered on inciting racial hatred and violence toward women, devoutly religious people, and anyone who didn't fit a very narrow-minded, bigoted view of the world. Some of his less heinous jokes included—

"I have heard that men in the fire service have a particular approach with their women. They like to find them hot and leave them wet…"

"A few first responder buddies, be they cops, E.M.T.s, or firefighters, like to sneak the word "This-Bitch" into the radio conversations when

the fine ladies at dispatch have upset them for one thing or another. You can just hear it… Dispatch to Engine Nine, Dispatch to Car Six… Yes, This-Bitch, this is Engine Nine/Car Six, go ahead."

"You overhear people all the time in bars or restaurants; they get mad because cops, ambulances and fire trucks can speed, like drive crazy speeds on emergency calls, and they get a ticket if they creep just over the limit. Talk about jealousy. You know what, it's called an emergency for a reason, you do know that, right? You know what, wait until it's your fucking emergency, and we'll tell the ambulance or the fire crew to take their time and enjoy their coffee or sandwich before they leave. Hello, heaven calling…"

One after the other, the people around the shocked quartet jeered and cheered Nathan's jokes. The four firefighters sat there in absolute silence. As he took a bow and prepared to leave the stage, they quickly discussed whether they should go before he noticed them. Clarissa was steadfast that she wanted to confront him about his routine, although she stopped short of confessing that evening had reignited her concerns about some of Nathan's previous actions at work. He slowly walked down the steps at the side of the stage, grabbed his jacket and headed to the bar; he had intended to speak to the people he usually did after a show. He never got that far. Nathan was about halfway across the room when he looked up and saw his workmates in the corner. His initial reaction was a combination of horror that they'd seen his routine, concern about how they would react and outright anger that they'd encroached on his personal life. Clarissa never beat around the bush, and she was the first of his colleagues to speak when he reached their table.

"Nath, errm… wow. We had no idea that you regularly did stand-up comedy, and when Tom saw the poster out front yesterday, we wanted to surprise you by coming along to support you. Your routine was, well, a bit out there for my taste. I don't know about you guys?" she asked as she gestured to the other three for back-up.

"I gotta say, Nathan, you have my admiration for getting up on stage to perform like that, but I can't say it appealed to my sense of humor either," said Peter.

Nathan's concern was ratcheting up by the second. The things he joked about were never meant for the people he worked with, and now he had to engage in a serious case of damage limitation.

"I'm sorry you didn't find it funny, guys; if you had mentioned you were thinking of coming, I would have suggested it probably wasn't your cup of tea. This was the first place I found that did an impromptu stand-up comedy evening, and having been up on stage a few times, I decided to continue performing here until I got more confident. I take it you all understand that you have to play to the crowd you're performing to… right?"

"Well, those in here certainly liked the content of your jokes. If I am being honest, I am surprised you decided to start off here and then stuck around. The people in here must have some pretty unpleasant political views; surely you could have found somewhere else to start?" probed Doug.

Their reaction was starting to feel like a personal attack to Nathan; he knew he had to tread really carefully.

"Hey, you know, this was the first place I saw hosting one, so… I came along. I gave it a go, tried to play up to the type of subjects the crowd wanted, and it's given me a foundation to work from. There is nothing more to it than that," Nathan persisted.

"Listen, it's not for us to judge what you do in your spare time. My only advice would be to try to find a new place sooner rather than later. Being here, joking about the sort of things you did and the way you did it, that does you no favors," warned Clarissa. "Also, Nathan, you need to be careful; this sort of thing can sometimes reflect badly on the station itself, causing unwanted scrutiny, and you don't want that. Well done for being able to get up there in the first place, honestly, I mean that, but I think I am going to head home now. I doubt the headline comic will indulge in humor that I like. You have a good night, Nathan."

"Tom, Peter… what about you?" asked Doug.

The other three also confirmed they were going to head home as well.

"Okay, listen, thanks for coming out. Please, just remember, I play to the audience in front of me… it's not like I really think that. I hope you get that," he implored as they grabbed their coats and headed for the exit.

"Yeah, we know that, buddy," confirmed Tom, with a worrying lack of sincerity.

Once they had gone, Nathan went back to the guys he knew at the bar. Despite their insistence that he should "ignore the bastards", his colleagues' reaction weighed heavily on his mind. Once the final comic had finished his routine, Nathan wished everyone a good weekend and caught a taxi home.

As he lay in bed that night, his mind was awash with worry that the quartet from work might start to question his morals, his political views, his previous actions and maybe even his motives. Having already raised an official statement about his negligent treatment at the football game, Clarissa was now his biggest concern; he tried to shrug it off by thinking that if she became too much of a problem, maybe she might have to meet an accident as well. The best way to avoid exacerbating the situation was to get back to his dark web activities, and that was exactly what he intended to do.

A couple of nights later, Nathan decided upon the next blackhat hacker he wanted to hire. It had taken a few days as he wanted to make sure he got the right person because his latest illegal information-gathering mission involved both a captain, Justin Anderson, and a colonel, Steven Cross. He provided

NothingOffTheTable with all the information they required to hack the various military servers where the reports from Anderson and Cross could be found.

Due to the increased sensitivity of the documents, NOTT wanted $60k in cryptocurrency to steal the requested information. To get everything he asked for, Nathan didn't care if it cost him $100k, he could happily have paid double the asking fee. To ensure dedication from the hacker, Nathan offered to pay an additional $10k if the person could provide anything above and beyond the official files that the two senior officers would have submitted. Taking just two days, Nathan was ecstatic when NOTT went well beyond his original remit by providing not only the documentation he wanted from the military mainframes, but numerous files from the home computers of both officers. It was a genuine pleasure for him to immediately transfer the funds to the cyber-criminal, and as agreed, he happily added the additional bonus for a job well done.

Nathan spent the next two nights wading through reams of reports that dealt with the mission where he was captured and its aftermath. Already knowing that Lt. Robertson had submitted documentation stating that he knew there was a very good chance that his staff sergeant was still alive when he ordered the retreat, Nathan was desperate to find out how his senior officers reacted. What he found out left him even more astonished!

Countless reports from both Anderson and Cross stated they had received and read all the official documents from Robertson. They were both fully aware that it was not only highly likely that the insurgents had captured Nathan, but that they would be torturing him for information. They accepted recommendations from several sources, including Robertson, that changes should be made to all codes, procedures, and deployments that Nathan knew about. In the days that followed, when asked whether a rescue mission should be implemented, not by Robertson but by other marines, including Dwayne, both men repeatedly declined the requests as they felt Nathan's life was not worth risking other marines in a rescue attempt. The fact they would have to find him first—given it was likely the insurgents would move him to another location quickly—was another issue that contributed to the decision.

That alone was impossible for Nathan to stomach, that his senior commanders decided his life wasn't worth saving, but later documentation from Anderson's home computer proved to be far worse. Around six months after the failed operation, a selection of private communications confirmed that contacts in Afghanistan informed Anderson that an American matching Nathan's description was being seriously tortured and, on two occasions, the informant even provided the location where he was being held. Other files indicated that Anderson initially tried to bury the new information about Nathan and his ongoing horrific situation. One reason for this was that he didn't want to risk the lives of other soldiers. However, Anderson's private records showed that his main concern was an overriding desire to avoid the negative publicity and fallout in the press that would come once they reported the story.

He concluded that both Robertson and himself would likely be publicly slaughtered for their decisions to leave behind an American soldier in a conflict zone. The fact they failed to launch a rescue mission and the subsequent torture of Nathan would only intensify the media scrutiny. Anderson decided it was better to withhold the latest information and hope the situation would quietly resolve itself. A few months later, covert operatives warned Anderson that it was inevitable that his superiors, including Cross, would find out from other sources. At that point, he did inform Colonel Cross about the "updated intel" regarding Nathan's predicament, but it was again concluded by both men that Nathan was not a high enough value target to deserve the large-scale rescue that would be required. When Anderson raised official worries about the potential public-relations disaster, Cross responded by saying that the military and Department of Defense would ensure the most damning evidence fell under the guise of highly classified material.

Cross's personal files corroborated that he was then complicit in withholding the information about Nathan from the highest echelons of the military above him. From his reports, it seemed Cross was unaware of the lengths that Anderson had already gone to in order to avoid escalating the intel, covering his ass with vague confessions of making decisions at his level. Cross was confident they could keep a lid on the press, but there was always the risk of a whistleblower or that maybe Nathan even knew his dire situation and whereabouts had been reported back. How would it look if he announced at a press conference that during his captivity he was secretly told that the U.S. Military knew where he was and failed to act?

In something of a mirror image, Anderson was unsure how Cross would react, and Cross, in turn, was uncertain about what action his superiors might take. Therefore, he concluded, much like Anderson, the risk of further loss of life was the prime concern and negated any possible rescue. With the decision made, he didn't need to run it up the chain of command. At the rank he was, Cross obviously assumed his decision was final and regardless of any new information, the matter was closed. Even when a C.I.A. deep cover operative provided Cross with Nathan's latest situation and location, he simply buried it in his own files.

Nathan wasn't sure if there was a word that adequately described how he felt once he had read through everything the hacker had provided. Apoplectic was a good start. If they had simply run the information up through the ranks, as they should have, and the most senior officials decided his rescue wasn't worth the lives of other men, he could probably have stomached that. He might have even accepted it if Anderson and Cross had made the same decision at their level. What he couldn't forgive was that both men were more concerned with their publicity and how they might be viewed in the press than they were with the lives of their men. That was absolutely unacceptable. However, it had now provided Nathan with the perfect idea of how to seek revenge against Anderson.

CHAPTER 10

The information that Nathan discovered in the hacked files weighed on his mind considerably. It was impossible for him to comprehend how two senior officers could effectively throw one of their own to the wolves because they were worried about how it would look in the press. The decision didn't involve some major Hollywood star or big-name musician who would lose a massive role or record deal if certain information leaked about their transgressions. This was a man's life, a soldier they left to be tortured and most likely killed, just so they wouldn't have to answer difficult questions. The argument about the lives of other soldiers in a rescue mission slowly began to fade from Nathan's psyche. He knew that played a factor and could understand it, but not enough to exonerate either man.

It would have proved a difficult time had that been the only thing Nathan was mentally dealing with, but things at work had also taken a turn for the worst. Word had spread throughout the station about the content of his stand-up routine and the type of people who hung out at the venue he performed in. It would have been foolish to hope that his four colleagues would say nothing, but it seemed they had spoken to everyone, from the part-time backups to the station commander. A couple of days later, maybe giving everything a chance to calm down, Capt. Mitchell called Nathan into his office.

"Nathan, it has come to my attention from other crew members that in your private time you have been performing stand-up comedy routines in a bar across town," began Mitchell.

Here we go, thought Nathan as he sat across the desk.

"It's not for me to dictate what you can and can't do when off-duty, but your actions do reflect on this station and the service in general. I understand the material you performed contained numerous jokes that were at best unpleasant and at worst downright abhorrent."

"Sir, with respect, I do not make any mention of this station or my actual job, and it's not like the tavern broadcasts my show on television or the net," highlighted Nathan. "I do understand the other members of the station didn't appreciate the material, but they are not regulars at the bar."

"Actually, that is as much my concern as what you said. I am aware of that place and the sort of people who frequent it. Frankly, I would be concerned if I was made aware one of my staff even drank there, let alone indulged in the sort of bigoted humor that you delivered on stage," continued Mitchell.

"Sir, I appreciate that aspect, and as I told Clarissa and the others, it was the first place that I came across that was small and did impromptu stand-up comedy nights. I am merely performing there to find my feet. That is their humor, so that is what I deliver, it is not like I believe or think in that way." There was his first lie, and he quickly followed it up with another. "I'm feeling confident enough to now start looking for another, slightly larger venue and when I do, my material will change to suit that audience."

He hoped that was enough to placate the captain and bring the matter to a quick close... with him at least.

"Okay. I can't demand you cease performing there, but if it continues for much longer, I will be forced to take action. I can't be seen to condone that sort of behavior and insidious humor from someone in your position. Frankly, I am more than a little troubled that a man as intelligent as you even considered it would be acceptable given your profession. I will not make an official record of this, but I suggest you make some changes to your personal life rather quickly. Dismissed."

Nathan's teeth clamped down on the inside of his lip. As far as he was concerned, as long as he didn't shout it from the rooftops, what difference did it make? Did telling a racist joke mean he wouldn't treat someone with a different skin color? Of course it didn't. Now, if the person was scum and hurt others, he might treat that person in his own special way, but it would have nothing to do with his skin color. Afghans… yes, he hated them, but that had nothing to do with their skin color; it was where they came from. Nathan was absolutely indignant and saw nothing wrong with his actions. He'd bought himself some breathing room, so would deal with his comedic issues later. In the meantime, he just wanted to focus on his day job, and privately fulfill his desire to seek retribution against Anderson and Cross.

Mitchell wasn't the only one who seemed to have serious misgivings about Nathan's private life. From the moment he walked into the station after the others had seen his performance, everyone started to behave slightly differently around him. It wasn't overt or outright obvious, just a subtle wariness and the odd conversation that would abruptly stop when he walked in the room. He put up with it for a few days, but in the end, he simply couldn't stand it any longer. The next morning, he asked Mitchell to call a station-wide meeting because he wanted to address the rest of his colleagues. The captain didn't think it was a good idea, but he reluctantly agreed. An hour later, Mitchell explained that he'd gathered everyone together at the request of Nathan, who had something to say. He shuffled to the side, and Nathan rose from his chair and stepped to the front.

"Listen, I know there has been some concern about my stand-up comedy hobby, and I totally understand your reservations. I have had a few days to think about it, and I can see why your opinions of me might have changed due to what you witnessed. As I told you all, my association with the Glass was merely a means to an end. I want to try a different way of performing in a couple of weeks, and that will be my last show there. I will then be seeking a new venue and a new clientele that will hopefully appreciate the sort of less offensive humor that we all find funny. Once I get a new gig, you'll be the first to know. I ask you all again, please do not judge me on the content of that show. It is no more representative of my opinions than if you were judged poorly because you went to the cinema to watch a film about white supremacists or the K.K.K. Please judge me on my actions and not words spoken to a bunch of small-minded rednecks in a bar."

He didn't miss the irony when he asked them not to judge him simply based on what he'd said to a select group of people. His words in the Glass were far more truthful and representative than anything he'd just said to them. The meeting seemed to have the desired effect, for the most part, and the majority of people were acting more normal within a couple of days… everyone except Clarissa. Her skepticism about his previous actions, both at the bar and as a first responder, and the sincerity of his regret continued unabated. She remained just the right side of the point where he would have to consider taking "action" against her.

The next couple of weeks became a bit of a repetitive blur for Nathan. He was on-shift almost every day, and his professional first responder life became a haze of call-outs and mind-numbing quiet periods. It didn't escape his attention that Clarissa worked exactly the same days as he did, and she rarely let him out of her sight when they were called out to a scene.

The majority of the incidents they attended involved people that Nathan had no issue with… they weren't bad people doing questionable things… well, not all of them.

There was a fire in a garage where a man had to jump from the upper window and broke his ankle. When it became obvious that he was a wife-beater, Nathan managed to surreptitiously worsen the break and even cause additional damage to his ligaments. The team attended a warehouse fire, and the firm in question were well-known for ripping people off and refusing refunds, so Nathan did his best to ensure there was as much damage to stock as possible. His only regret was that none of the owners were in the building at the time.

Having just put out a car that caught fire due to mechanical failure, dispatch immediately redirected Nathan's team to the banks of the Potomac River. A boat had capsized, and a man was in distress. He'd gone under literally seconds before they arrived, and as Nathan stripped down to dive in, one bystander declared they should let him drown because the man was a known scam artist who swindled money from old people. Nathan had read about a few unsuccessful cases against him, so that was exactly what he did. Underwater, Nathan saw the man's final few seconds of consciousness, and he simply floated there and watched. Having come up for air a couple of times, he dragged the body from the water when he was confident the man was dead. It helped that he was responsible for resuscitation, and all attempts failed to revive the man.

The team attended a couple of bizarre call-outs during those weeks. One was a house fire that was started by a woman who tried to burn a large spider with a lighter and an aerosol can; she burned both the sink and then the curtains, which quickly caused a large blaze. Another afternoon they were called out to a hotel, where Nathan had to cut free a naked man handcuffed to the bed; his mistress had left him there after she had found out he was married. Ludicrous group initiations were another semi-regular occurrence, from people stuck to the toilet seat by superglue to freeing someone who'd stuck their arm/leg/head/penis in an unusual place or object. Along the same lines, Nathan couldn't claim that rescuing a gorgeous half-naked lady who'd got her finger jammed in the shower screen door was a hardship.

Just when he thought everything was somewhat back to normal, and he could revert his main focus back to his plans for Anderson and Cross, Nathan overheard a conversation that wasn't meant for his ears. He'd left the station as usual that night and was almost halfway home when he realized he'd left his cell phone in his locker. By the time he got back, most of the others had also left for the night. The light was on in the captain's office, but that was far from unusual. He heard Mitchell's voice when he first re-entered the station, and not wanting to disturb him if he was in a conference call, Nathan quietly made his way to the locker room. It was then that he heard Clarissa's voice. The two of them were in quite a serious discussion based on the tone of their voices, but Nathan couldn't quite hear what they were saying. He stealthily moved closer and was able to pick up snippets of their conversation.

He heard Clarissa mention things like, "...could it have been on purpose?...odd, random events that seem to happen around him...is there more to it than just a poor choice in humor?" and even, "...look deeper into his call-outs, let's see if there is an unethical issue."

Nathan didn't need to hear everything to know exactly who Clarissa was talking about.

He also picked up on parts of Mitchell's side of the conversation, replies such as "...are you sure you're not imagining it?...serious accusations to make...if that's true, there are major questions to answer."

Not wanting to alert the conspiring pair that he'd overheard them, Nathan quietly made his way out of the station. The last thing he made out was Mitchell confirming that he was happy for Clarissa to "carry out an informal, discrete investigation to see if there is any wrongdoing."

On his way home, he contemplated how to deal with the situation. He was confident he'd covered his tracks, but as an ex-marine, he was aware that intel was key. Via the dark web, Nathan purchased a couple of minuscule listening devices, and secretly placed them in Mitchell's room. Over the next fortnight, he recorded four different late-night conversations between Clarissa and Mitchell. During the first two, she provided verbal reports about where she'd looked, what she'd investigated, and that she would continue digging. During the fourth meeting, she confessed that despite her extensive research, most of which she'd done while off duty, she had been unable to uncover any actual evidence of wrongdoing. When he heard that, Nathan sat back with a satisfied smile.

"Take that, you sneaky bitch," he muttered.

He knew there was nothing he could do about her right now; any form of accident or untoward event was a non-starter. Unfortunately, that meant she would continue to keep him under intense scrutiny, and did so by ensuring she always worked the same shifts and the same incidents. Clarissa rarely let him out of her sight, and he was fine with that at first, but his frustration quickly began to build. He was forced to properly treat three people in two days that he felt deserved a different outcome. Throughout every call-out, she watched him like a hawk and gave him absolutely no leeway to try anything. His irritation grew with each and every incident where he couldn't act because of her close observation. He kept telling himself that she couldn't watch him intently forever, and eventually she might become so preoccupied with him that maybe she would be the one that made mistakes.

The pressure valve got partially released when his team, plus another from a different station and four ambulances, were called out to a massive pile-up on Interstate 66. There was a total of fifteen casualties spread across the six wrecked vehicles. The male and female occupants of one car were already dead, while the male and two females in a second car were in a very serious condition. The two parents and their daughter in the third car were also in a bad way, as were the family of five in the fourth vehicle. The fire crews immediately got to work trying to cut free the occupants of those three vehicles.

The remaining two cars had one male occupant each. The police had already established that one of them was responsible for the crash. He had been drunk driving, lost control and swerved across two lanes. The others crashed when they slammed on their brakes or tried to avoid him. The male in the final vehicle had suffered some relatively nasty facial injuries, but nothing that was considered life-threatening. One officer at the scene quietly joked with his colleagues that their jobs might be easier if they left the "blood-sucking defense lawyer" to his own fate.

Nathan was desperate to work on the man responsible for the collision, or at least the lawyer, but Clarissa was already ahead of him. She quickly suggested to Lt. Spencer that Nathan should concentrate on the two seriously injured families, where his extensive trauma knowledge would be invaluable. He agreed, and assigned Nathan to help the ambulance teams who were treating the two families in the third and fourth vehicles, while Doug and Clarissa focused on cutting them free. Flitting between the two vehicles and helping the ambulance teams, with Clarissa keeping an ever watchful eye, he acted magnificently and was responsible for saving at least two of the children in those cars.

Taking a momentary breather, Nathan noticed that there was just one fireman working to free the lawyer from his car. That man deserved a small taste of Nathan's justice, if only for his "Jud$e Me" license plate, let alone for all the criminals he'd helped over the years. He suggested to Spencer that the two of them should assist their fellow responder from the other station to free the man from his car. When the others were not looking,

Nathan managed to trip the airbag that had previously failed to deploy, and it instantly exploded in the lawyer's face. The impact knocked the man out and also removed four of his teeth. Considering the lawyer's vain appearance and his protestations that they shouldn't ruin his suit, losing four teeth seemed a just reward. It had worked perfectly because Nathan had timed it exactly when the other fireman was using the hydraulic tool to cut the man free, making it look like the vibrations caused the accident. He did it in full view of Spencer to ensure Clarissa could have no cause to question the incident. Nathan couldn't deny he was thrilled with himself, especially when he later found that it caused a fractured jaw as well.

That just left the drunk driver. Nathan struggled to maintain his composure because he was desperate to punish the man. The lawyer was just a bonus, but the man who caused all this death and destruction needed to pay. Every time it looked like an opportunity might open up for Nathan to get involved with that vehicle, Clarissa shouted for his help and dragged his moment of retribution away from him. During the two hours they were on scene, Nathan ended up making a couple of small mistakes when treating the families due to his ever-increasing urge to harm the drunk driver. He missed a less obvious side injury in one child, and then administered a dosage of painkiller that was slightly too high to one of the parents. Luckily for Nathan, it was Doug who spotted the error. He was unaware of Clarissa's deep-seated worries about Nathan's behavior, and also willing to give his colleague the benefit of the doubt when it came to his comedy routine. He quietly informed Nathan about the two mistakes, in quick succession, then told him he understood he had a lot on his mind and that the matter ended there, unless the mistakes continued then he would have to report them. At the time, Clarissa was pulling one of the parents from the other car, and though she kept looking over, she saw nothing of concern and was none the wiser. Try as he might, Nathan was unable to get anywhere near the drunk driver. He was eventually taken to hospital, accompanied by two police officers, and Nathan's chance to make him pay for recklessly killing two people was over.

The beast of vengeance consumed Nathan that night. He was ferociously angry that Clarissa had robbed him of the chance to punish the drunken man. For a few moments, he genuinely contemplated going to her house and dealing with "that fucking whore" once and for all, by beating her to a pulp. He'd put her in a coma that she'd never recover from… just a break-in gone bad! A modicum of self-control quickly appeared, and he reminded himself that lashing out at her would likely bring an end to his retaliatory mission against Anderson and Cross.

To satisfy his thirst and scratch that retribution itch, he got to work on his plan to destroy Captain Anderson. He was a married family man with four kids. Nathan didn't want to kill him straight away, that would be too easy; he wanted Anderson to suffer. As he was so preoccupied with what the press thought of him, Nathan decided to destroy Anderson in the most public way possible. He employed a hacker with a very unsavory reputation, even amongst the dark web's lawless community. Nathan agreed to a contract worth $75k with the cyber-criminal known only as BadmanBruce99. His task was to create a fake trail on all of Anderson's devices that would prove the military man was obsessed by extreme pornography. The hacker loaded up his computers, both private and professional, plus both his cell phones with gigabytes of extreme and horrendous material. BB99 promised the stuff he'd left would leave the world's most perverted mind in absolute shock.

A couple of nights later, Nathan arranged for an anonymous tip to be made to both the civilian and military police, and they descended on Anderson's house. He was immediately arrested and charged with multiple disturbing counts that related to the most extreme forms of pornography. Nathan had found a perfect spot in the woods behind his victim's house, sitting camouflaged up in a tree, and he sat there, evening after evening, watching Anderson's life implode. His wife left him straight away and took the children with her, while the marines placed him on indefinite leave, the likelihood being he would be dishonorably discharged before a criminal conviction and jail time. Nathan savored each and every destructive moment as he watched Anderson's life torn apart.

CHAPTER 11

Anyone with a conscience would have brought a halt to the suffering of Justin Anderson. A second anonymous tip confirming that the evidence had all been fabricated would have brought the whole horrific affair to a close. Nathan Profit didn't have a conscience, and he felt no remorse and no sympathy for the man who had left him for dead.

Each night when he finished work, Nathan drove home and quickly ate his meal before heading out again. To him, it was nothing more unusual than the man down the street coming home and walking his dog every night. The once courteous, considerate, and caring marine was so full of venom and hostility that his mind saw nothing wrong with what he was doing. With his night vision goggles, camo gear and recording equipment ready, Nathan again drove to the edge of the woodland area near Anderson's house. He switched between three trees, just in case the regularity of using one position became too comfortable and he made a mistake that was spotted by Anderson.

His evening viewing was akin to someone going to a drive-in movie; he would sit back in the tree, quietly munch on the odd snack, enjoy a non-alcoholic drink, and savor the visual spectacle in front of him. After the first few nights, Nathan decided to start recording what he witnessed, so he could replay it again at his leisure. He was almost annoyed with himself that he hadn't thought of it from the beginning because that would have given him the ability to rewatch the very best bits of Anderson's downfall. The initial few days was the period that included the arguments with his wife, where she threw things at him and called him the most unspeakable names, her walkout with the kids, and the various police searches of his house. Nathan got a real thrill watching the officers literally rip his house to pieces looking for evidence. What made it all the more special was the fact that Nathan knew there was nothing for the authorities to find. He did toy with the idea of paying someone to break in and place a few "items of interest" in concealed places, but he felt someone like Anderson wouldn't make such an obvious mistake. He was sure the police knew that too, but they still had to search his house, and watching his home get totally wrecked was extremely satisfying for Nathan. How he would have loved to be able to enjoy those glorious moments over and over again; instead, he would have to settle for remembering them in years to come.

Now isolated from everyone, not only his family but any contact with others due to the authorities confiscating his cell phones and computers, Nathan watched Anderson sink into the pit of despair. He watched him drinking heavily each night, and he even resorted to taking illegal drugs, such as cannabis and heroin, that a local dealer chucked into the hedge near Anderson's front door. Nathan wanted to strip everything away from his ex-commanding officer, so he tipped off the police, who were there to arrest the dealer one evening. It was a double win; Anderson denied something else and another piece of trash off the streets.

He watched Anderson walking tearfully around the house, picking up photos and bursting into tears again as he slumped to the floor. That slightly irritated Nathan as he couldn't see what his victim was doing. Every evening, from his perch up high, he witnessed Anderson's rapid descent into oblivion. With his illegal drugs taken away, Anderson drank more and more, and he often passed out cold on the floor or on the sofa, at which point Nathan would go home. Part of him wanted to stay all night to see if he went into any sort of meltdown in the very early hours, but having made a couple of mistakes during the major M.V.A. incident, he couldn't allow a repeat of that due to extreme tiredness. He contemplated leaving some recording equipment, so he could capture any delicious moments that happened during the daytime, but swiftly decided that was a risk too far; what if it was discovered by accident? As tempting as it was, especially if that would grant him extra footage of the police interviews, he settled for watching him each night from his trio of vantage points.

Anderson continued to rapidly deteriorate. It was obvious he was drinking ludicrous amounts and was working his way through about two bottles a night. Nathan had no idea how he was getting hold of so much alcohol, although he didn't really care about that. Taking away the drugs had increased Anderson's pain, and that was enjoyable, but he didn't want to remove his alcohol as well; his nightly drunken stupor was providing Nathan with too much entertainment. It was around the middle of the second week when Anderson reached the stage that Nathan had been waiting for. It was just before midnight, and the utterly disgraced captain was once again absolutely hammered. Slumped in a chair watching some random film, Nathan saw him take another swig before picking up a bottle of pills. He hadn't made up his mind how he wanted the situation to end. The longer Anderson suffered, the happier he was, but there was also something quite alluring about the possibility of his victim becoming so broken that he took his own life.

Nathan was so far gone from the man he used to be that he couldn't even see the connection between himself and the man he was torturing. He had become so bitter, so twisted, and so vicious that it completely obscured something so obvious. If he had genuinely stopped and thought about it, the man on the other side of the windows was in a similarly desperate state to the one he endured on his return from Afghanistan. In the weeks after he found out about Lisa and her new life, it had been Nathan sat there with countless bottles of booze and numerous boxes of pills. In a mirror image, it was him sitting in a chair and contemplating the idea of ending his own life. Some of the worst criminals that became famous throughout history had the occasional bout of sympathy for their victims, but there wasn't a shred of that, nor decency, left in Nathan.

It soon became too much for Anderson to endure, and even the alcohol could no longer numb the pain he felt. Late one evening, Nathan watched, almost totally captivated, as Anderson sat in a chair with a rope in his hands. With his eyes full of tears, he slowly tied it into a noose. Nathan had a decision to make; would he be satisfied if Anderson ended his torment by taking his life, the final price paid, or did his vengeance demand that this pitiful example of a man should continue to suffer indefinitely? If the latter, he had to act quickly and find a way to stop Anderson without giving himself away. He looked at the desperate man through the window and contemplated what to do next; in the end, he decided to do nothing.

About twenty minutes later, with Nathan recording the whole thing through the window, Anderson tied the rope through a beam in the room and stood on a chair he had just placed underneath it. He paused for a moment, no doubt looking at a picture or something on the wall, then placed the noose around his neck. Seconds later, he kicked the chair away and hung himself. As his body thrashed and kicked about, the rope choking the last vestiges of life from him, all Nathan did was zoom in with his camera. A minute or so later, he hung motionless—Captain Justin Anderson was dead. Nathan wasn't sure how long he just sat there looking at the lifeless remains, it must have been twenty minutes or more, and he couldn't explain why he was drawn to just staring through the window at his dead former comrade. The only thing he was sure about was the sensation of righteousness that flowed through every part of him. He took another minute to memorize the scene in every detail before climbing down from his perch for the last time. Before he left, Nathan carefully swept the area to ensure he'd left no clues or evidence that someone had been watching the house. Once he was certain there was nothing to give away his nightly vigil, he contently made his way home.

When he got back, Nathan took fifteen minutes to rewatch some of the footage he'd taken that night. At one point, the video perfectly captured the agony and fear in Anderson's face just a few seconds before he passed out. Nathan paused it on his laptop screen. He hadn't really noticed it at the time, but now he just stared at the freeze-frame image. That man had left him to die an awful death in Afghanistan, and while his torture didn't remotely match the years of hell Nathan endured, that look of terror in Anderson's eyes at that moment provided Nathan with some restitution. The only remaining question in his mind was how quickly would the authorities discover the body?

Two days later, Dwayne called Nathan and asked whether he could pop over; his friend obviously agreed with his request. Dwayne spent nearly two hours telling Nathan all about the charges against Anderson, how his wife had left him with the kids, and that the police found his dead body earlier that afternoon when they turned up to ask more questions. Dwayne appeared genuinely stunned by everything that had happened, and Nathan had to work extremely hard to appear just as shocked by the chain of events. When Dwayne mentioned that he was starting to feel their old unit was cursed—Nathan's ordeal, Robertson's accident and now Anderson's suicide—it somewhat vindicated his decision not to go after the lower ranked marines. Had some of them also encountered unpleasant outcomes, it would probably have caused opinions to change from a difficult set of coincidences into the realm of the odds were too high for it to be random. Before Dwayne left, his friend suggested they both raised a drink to Anderson; he wanted Nathan to make the toast and confessed he found his ensuing words wonderfully touching. Nathan couldn't remember the last time he was pleased to see Dwayne go home, but it had been such an emotional couple of weeks and the effort of enforced sadness was simply too draining. Due to the awful accusations and charges filed against Captain Anderson, almost no one showed up at his funeral. Dwayne was in two minds, but Nathan talked him into going because he wanted to go himself, whether it was to gloat one more time or feel the strange, now alien sensation of doing the right thing, he didn't know. In the end, the two marines, plus Colonel Cross, were the only ones who showed up.

The demise of Anderson left Nathan on a high. All but one of the people he deemed responsible for his ordeal had now paid a price for their decisions and inaction to save him. There was a serious chance that once he turned his attention to Cross, that people might start asking questions. As much as he wanted to make them all pay, he wasn't sure that he wanted it to be a suicide mission. After all, what good would that do? He wouldn't be around to enjoy the final outcome of his extensive planning and meticulously carried out acts of vengeance. It wasn't as if Cross would be going anywhere in the near future. His previous posting in Afghanistan was the senior officer's final overseas command, so bar retiring somewhere on a whim, he would likely be around Washington, D.C. for some time to come. He had plenty of time, and there was no need to rush the grand finale of his plan.

He was now free to return all his attention to his paramedic role, regardless of whether it involved helping people or harming the unworthy. His actions against Anderson had released all the pressure and pent-up frustration that had quickly built through his inability to act when he felt it was warranted. Nathan knew that Clarissa would still be a thorn in his side, and he had to keep in mind that her unproven crusade against him had resulted in Captain Mitchell paying closer attention to everything he did. There were ways and means, he told himself, but next time, when the resentment spilled over, he knew he could recall the calmness he felt sitting in the tree as Anderson hung from his noose.

According to Nathan's warped view of life, he'd had a good couple of weeks and fate was about to drop another gold-plated opportunity right in his lap. During a fairly quiet afternoon, the station received an urgent call-out from dispatch to attend the scene of a major house fire. They were one of three stations that were sent to deal with the blaze because it involved a fairly large building. While en-route, Mitchell came over the radio to confirm that the residential home in question belonged to Larry Brooks, a wealthy property tycoon who recently became a U.S. senator. There was a collective groan around the fire truck when the crew heard his name.

Even Nathan was aware of Brooks because there was a lot of consternation and unhappiness when he was elected the previous year as the senator for Vermont. Over the past decade, there had been multiple court cases brought against Brooks due to his apparently disreputable deals, dodgy ethics, and his predisposition to swiftly evicting vulnerable people regardless of the reason, even if it was due to the failure of his own business ventures. He was widely disliked and yet the courts had only found him guilty on one occasion, and even that was a technicality. He may not have been able to smile on the outside, but Nathan was overjoyed within… now, he just had to find a way to get alone with Brooks.

Whether by luck or cosmic design, a car crash involving three vehicles delayed the other two trucks, so Nathan's team were the first and only fire crew on-site. Normally, Lt. Spencer would take charge of such a high-profile incident, but they didn't know about the senator's involvement until they were halfway there. Doug, Tom, and Nathan got to work with the hoses, while Clarissa and Tom turned their attention to the ladders. The fire was violently roaring on the upper level of the house and in the few minutes they were there, the ground-floor ceiling collapsed and ignited the rest of the house. Out of nowhere, there were cries of help from the rooftop. Nathan looked up and saw it was the senator. His wife and children were standing outside the house because they had been able to flee before the fire got out of control, but the blaze had trapped Brooks upstairs. In an act of desperation, he'd climbed onto the roof via a balcony. The scene was quickly unfolding, and nobody, not even Clarissa, raised any objection when Nathan subtly took control and started issuing orders.

He placed Peter in his usual position by the truck, monitoring water flow and giving everyone visual updates, and suggested Clarissa should focus on fighting the ever-growing fire downstairs. It suited her physical stature better and was an obvious choice, but with all that had happened, he was certain she would resist; to his genuine surprise, she agreed and got to work. He instructed Tom to direct his hose at the upper tier from the ground in an attempt to prolong the life of the roof before it collapsed. That left Doug to alternate the direction of his hose between both floors. With his colleagues right in the thick of it, that left Nathan alone on the ladder to rescue Senator Brooks.

Once at the top, Nathan could see that the senator was extremely frightened and clinging to the chimney. The roof was quite uneven, and he could tell that the flames underneath would soon weaken it to the point that it collapsed. He yelled down to Doug to bring him a fire pole, shouting loudly and clearly that he would use it to double-check the strength of the roof between himself and the senator. He made sure he asked if anyone had a better idea. Clarissa couldn't offer an alternative suggestion and called out that he needed to hurry because the flames underneath were ripping through the house.

"Senator… Senator Brooks… my name is Nathan Profit. I know you're scared but listen to me. I am going to use this pole to check the strength of the roof around you. That way, we can ascertain the safest route to get you to shuffle over to me. Do you understand?" Nathan informed him.

The petrified man on the roof confirmed he understood. What he didn't understand was that Nathan intended to do the exact opposite. From left to right, he whacked the pole down on the roof. There was no way the senator would have any idea what looked solid and what appeared to be close to giving way. It was quickly apparent that the roof on the right side was weakening. He whacked it a few more times. The dullness of the reverberations told Nathan it was severely unstable. Before he could carry out his plan, he wanted to make sure there was a witness near him.

"Clarissa, can you get up here with that other hose? I want you to direct it up past me onto the roof to cool it down before the senator climbs across it," he asked.

In her usual quick and unfussy manner, she was straight up the ladder and positioned just below Nathan. He made sure she had a good view of what was happening, but that his body partially obscured the section he was about to whack with the pole. She told Nathan it would be unwise to douse the roof for more than twenty seconds, and he quickly agreed. She directed the water and it splashed all over the tiles.

"Senator, let me check it again," he told Brooks.

Hitting the roof, he could tell that it was getting even weaker. The water had cooled the slates, but the weight of the liquid was now adding to the disastrous outcome. Had Clarissa been the one to test the stability of the roof, she would have known the right side was wrong, especially once doused, and directed the senator to the other side of the chimney. Unfortunately for Brooks, she wasn't the one assessing the roof.

Nathan banged the pole a couple more times, purposely just away from the route he was sending Brooks, so Clarissa could hear the solid thump.

"Does that sound sturdy enough to you, Clarissa?" he purposely inquired.

"Yeah, Nathan, that was a solid bang. Bring him down quickly, from the look of things through this window, we don't have long."

She was now complicit in the decision.

"Senator Brooks, I want you to slowly slide down this section of roof toward me. If I tell you to go back, do it quickly, okay?"

Brooks agreed again. He gradually let go of the chimney and began his apprehensive slide down the wet roofing slates.

"It doesn't feel solid," shouted Brooks.

"It's just fine, sir, trust me," urged Nathan with a genuine smile.

It was now difficult for Clarissa to hear because the other two engines and a pair of ambulances had just arrived with their sirens blaring. Spotting her looking away and unable to hear, he whacked the roof again.

"Just testing, sir... everything is fine, but please, hurry," instructed Nathan.

"Fireman, what's wrong with you, this part of the roof doesn't feel safe. Do you know what you're doing? Are you absolutely sure?" Brooks inquired with noticeable concern.

"Yes, sir, I know exactly what I'm doing..."

Brooks shuffled closer and was just about to reach the softest part of the roof. Nathan looked down at Clarissa, who was now engaged in directing her hose at the inferno in the room below, and it was clear she was completely distracted. He turned his gaze back to Brooks as the man inched closer. What the senator witnessed was an evil smile and a look of satisfaction.

"Here, sir, grab hold of this…"

Nathan lifted his pole, as high as possible without looking obvious, and dropped it in front of the senator. One hit was all he needed. The entire side of the roof suddenly collapsed, and Senator Brooks fell with it into the very heart of the fire. He was dead in seconds, if not quicker.

With fake yells of concern, Nathan pretended to rush down the ladder to see if he could fight his way through the blaze downstairs to "rescue" the politician. He forced both Tom and Doug to hold him back. Even Clarissa assured him there was nothing more he could do. As the lone fire crew at the scene, they had all done everything possible to save the senator, but it wasn't enough. It took the three teams nearly two hours to put the fire out. By the time it was over, there was nothing left but the burnt out walls. Somewhere in the blackened heart of the house was the charred remains of Senator Brooks. As he sat with his back to the building, Nathan allowed himself a quick, tiny smile. Thanks to his actions, that despicable man had got what he deserved.

Nathan maintained a somber mood when they returned to the station that night. A loss like that would haunt any fireman, and he made sure everyone saw how gutted he was to have got so close to saving the life of Senator Brooks. That night, he really wanted to go down to the Looking Glass, but having gone someway to repairing the damage caused by his workmates' surprise visit, he resisted the urge. Instead, he celebrated another job well done with a few drinks at home.

CHAPTER 12

There was an unpleasant surprise waiting for Nathan when he arrived at work the next morning. Due to Senator Brooks' very public profile, the fire service had assigned two investigators to carry out a thorough review of everything that happened the previous day. They had watched the body cam footage from every police officer at the scene, and now wanted to take statements from the station's firefighters who attended the fatal blaze. While the Washington Police Department had been wearing body cams since late 2016, the 2,800 cameras being the largest deployment of body cameras at the time, the capital's fire crews rarely wore them. Nathan was aware that his station did require at least one member at the incident to wear a cam, and that was usually the truck driver; the logic being that he was often stood by the engine and had a wide view of everything that was going on. Nathan was aware of this and had always been mindful of it whenever he did something nefarious.

The captain gave them his office to use as an interview room, and having watched the recording from Peter's body cam, they called the team in one by one. Nathan was the last to be interviewed, and having been responsible for the death of Brooks, many people might have viewed that as something to be worried about. It was one thing to lie to colleagues or the two senior firemen in the station, but investigators dealt with dishonest people all the time. They were trained to spot inconsistencies and the subtle physical traits that people did without realizing it when they gave false information. Nathan was so confident in his actions that it was easy for him to accurately portray the image of an innocent firefighter who tried his best to save a victim yet was also saddened that he failed to do so.

The two investigators repeatedly asked about the state of the roof, and why Nathan had told Brooks to make his way across a section that ultimately collapsed. He stuck to his story that he'd used his pole to test the roof's solidity, and mentioned a few times that his colleague, Clarissa, confirmed she thought it sounded solid enough from her position on the ladder. They showed Nathan the body cam footage, and he talked them through each minute of the rescue attempt. Peter had recorded the whole incident as normal, but Nathan's position on the ladder often obscured the senator from view because of the upward angle. He was in the room longer than the others, but that was to be expected given he was most involved with the unsuccessful rescue of Brooks.

The investigators spoke to everyone at least twice, and bar a couple of call-outs, the interviews carried on all day. As the afternoon slipped into the early evening, the investigators wrapped everything up. The captain knew one of them fairly well and asked for some quiet, unofficial feedback. He was told there were still lots of things to look into, such as evidence from the scene and other eyewitness statements, but based on the information they'd assessed from the police and his firefighters, he was confident that Mitchell's team had done everything correctly. The only question mark about their actions was that the other inspector felt Nathan could have climbed a rung or two higher to be able to physically reach the victim sooner, but accepted the potential risk of flames bursting through the window was adequate reason for the cautious approach. The investigation eventually concluded the fire and the senator's death were both accidental.

The next few weeks passed relatively slowly for Nathan, despite his station experiencing quite a busy period. When needed and where possible, he dished out his special treatment to a few undesirables, but the majority of the victims were innocent, everyday people with no filthy habits or harmful history that required his extracurricular attention. Clarissa remained ever vigilant around him and still had the odd meeting with Mitchell that he recorded, but he was supremely confident he had nullified any threat she posed.

The reason the weeks appeared to drag for Nathan was due to the fact he was eager to complete his campaign of revenge against the marines. There was now only one military person remaining alive that Nathan felt was responsible for his Afghanistan horrors—Colonel Steven Cross. At the end of the day, the buck stopped with the man at the top, and regardless of what Robertson and Anderson had done, Cross had still had opportunities to rescue Nathan and willfully decided against it. As far as he could tell, no one had made any link between the previous deaths, but to avoid even the remotest risk that someone could start putting the pieces together and place Cross under extra security, he forced himself to be patient and careful. The only question in his mind was about how he was going to do it. He didn't want to forgo his own life, so the logical suggestion was to create another accident using proxy anonymous contacts.

However, deep down, he still wanted to be directly responsible for the man's death, so he eventually came up with a more direct plan to plant bombs at the colonel's house. He would purchase the materials to make several explosive devices, then pay an online criminal to plant evidence at the home of a "questionable" citizen with Middle East links, using him as a fall guy for the bombs that Nathan would plant. He knew he could buy the ingredients through the dark web, but Nathan had always stipulated that his actions must involve as few people as possible. Therefore, he decided to obtain almost everything by his own means. Nathan was well aware how the authorities monitored suspicious purchases by the same person, so he was able to persuade his colleagues to pick up certain items for him because he had "a lot on" at the time. On their own, these seemed innocent enough, but they became deadly once combined with other items.

Just after Nathan had completed his shopping list and was about to move onto the planning stage, his team received a call-out to attend an emergency at the same school his daughter went to. If all five of his team had been on duty, he would have asked Mitchell if he could stay at the station because he didn't want to give Lisa an excuse to think he had used his job as an opportunity to see Charlotte unsupervised. Unfortunately, Doug was off sick, so the team was already at the minimum level they were allowed. Just to legally protect himself, Nathan asked his captain to provide a written statement that confirmed his place on the crew was a necessity; Mitchell understood his predicament and promised to add it straight away to his personnel file. The dispatch operator was able to provide extra information from the head teacher's 911 call just before the engine left the station.

The school had a retention pond that was surrounded by metal railings. There were two teachers on duty in the playground during lunch, but when they were dragged over the opposite side to break up a fight between several older pupils, a group of younger ones snuck through a broken rail and were playing near the pond. Two of them had fallen in and the teachers were in the process of rescuing them, but the school still wanted emergency services at the scene. The head teacher described the victims as an eight-year-old boy called Martin, and a seven-year-old girl called Jennifer.

Pretending to show deep concern because his daughter went to the school, but already knowing it involved two other children, Nathan did all he could to stall the engine's departure, keeping it just the right side of believable. The school was specifically for children with parents in the armed forces, and knowing his daughter was safe, Nathan's blind hatred of the military left him unconcerned about the well-being of another comrade's child. In his mind, they all bore some responsibility for the loss of his family. They were told an ambulance was on its way as well, but the fire crew would get there first.

When the engine arrived, they parked it as close to the pond as possible. From a distance, as he climbed out, Nathan observed two small groups of people surrounding two children who were on the floor. There were several teachers and four police officers already busy trying to save the lives of both children. Nathan could see the girl had blond hair, so he knew for sure it wasn't his own daughter. Clarissa and Tom immediately sprinted over to the scene, while Peter dug around in the engine to make sure any possible equipment they might need was on hand. Nathan wanted to delay helping as long as possible, so halfway to the group with the girl, he purposely tripped and pretended to bang his head on the floor. He sat up and paused, taking extra precious seconds to simulate being temporarily stunned, then jumped up and quickly made his way over to the now quite manic scene. Clarissa yelled at Nathan to come over and help her with the unconscious girl because he was the most medically qualified. Tom was already with the boy who'd regained consciousness.

As he rushed over and dropped to his knees, Clarissa was already leaning over the girl and giving her mouth-to-mouth resuscitation. He still couldn't see the child's face because Clarissa's head was in the way. Nathan knelt down and began to rummage in his bag for the equipment he needed, such as an ambu-bag/resuscitation-bag and oximeter. Having now reached the stage where any further delay would result in serious questions, Nathan turned to look at the patient. As Clarissa lifted her head to let him take over, he saw her face for the first time. Nathan Profit could have died right there on the spot. Staring up at him was the face of Charlotte.

"Fucking hell, that's my daughter… get out of the way," he screamed.

He literally shoved Clarissa aside and went into a blind panic. The person who'd provided the I.D. of the victim had got it horribly wrong and instead of a girl called Jennifer, it was his own precious Charlotte. How was he to know that his ex-wife had used a two-day dye on Charlotte's hair to turn it from mousy-brown to blond for a fancy dress party? Nathan worked frantically on his daughter.

"Clarissa, I'm sorry I just shoved you… please, help me, I'm begging you," implored Nathan.

By now, Peter had run over and helped with the male patient, so Tom stepped in to assist with Charlotte. Nathan's treatment became ever more frenzied, and in the end, Clarissa and Tom had to take control. They would physically treat her, and asked Nathan to stand back and simply direct them. Over and over, they repeated the cycle of breathing into her mouth four times, then pumping her chest to try to restart her heart. Within two minutes, the ambulance crew arrived and hurriedly took over. Clarissa and Tom put their arms around Nathan, and they eased him backward a couple of steps.

"Let them work, Nathan, there is nothing more we can do. They're as well-trained as you, you know that, let's just give them space," she tentatively suggested.

About six steps back, Nathan stood there motionless as the ambulance team fought to save his daughter's life. They tried everything from continued CPR to three jolts from a defibrillator, but Charlotte remained motionless on the floor. A second ambulance had arrived and was in the process of preparing to take the boy to a hospital. A paramedic from the second team came over to see if she could help. A minute later, they stopped the CPR.

"What are you doing? Why have you stopped? She hasn't come around yet… keep going!" Nathan yelled.

The lady who'd been working tirelessly on her for nearly ten minutes stood up and walked over to Nathan.

"Sir, I understand you are her father. I don't know what to say. No parent should go through or see this. I am so very sorry… we've done all we can… she's gone."

She turned to the other two paramedics, and they confirmed their agreement. The senior E.M.T. officially pronounced her dead a few seconds later. Nathan's emotions spilled over, and he dropped to his knees beside his daughter. Looking up at the sky, he let out a scream that was part shock and part rage. He picked up Charlotte and cradled her in his arms. Everyone bar Clarissa took a few steps back. She gave him several minutes, then tenderly kneeled next to him.

"Nathan, you need to let the ambulance team take her to the hospital. Come on, we'll get you back to the station, and then I'll drive you straight to the hospital if you want, so you can be with her for a while," she promised him.

At first, he refused to allow her body to be taken from his grasp, but Clarissa eventually persuaded him to allow the paramedics to lift her onto a bed and take her to the hospital. With everyone walking away from the pond, Nathan sat on the ground and just gazed at the water. It still hadn't sunk in that he'd just killed his beloved daughter because of his own inaction. They left him alone for about ten minutes, then Clarissa went and helped him to his feet. She did her best to put her arm around him, a far from easy task given his height. His steps toward the engine were stumbling shuffles. About halfway there, the head teacher came over; it was the most unwise decision he would make in his entire career.

"Mr. Profit. I just wanted to tell you how sorry I am. Charlotte was a lovely girl and we all adored her. I promise you; there will be a full investigation into what happened," he assured the grieving father.

"You didn't even know it was her. You gave us the wrong name… why didn't you tell us it was her? How does a teacher not know which child is in distress?" he mumbled.

"Come on, Nathan, this won't help anything," said Clarissa.

"Our thoughts are with you and your ex-wife, Mr. Profit," declared the principle.

Nathan took about two steps, then without warning, he spun around and launched a volley of furious punches to the teacher's face. As the man collapsed to the floor, Nathan dropped to his knees and punched him again and again. It took the entire fire crew—Tom, Peter, and Clarissa, plus three police officers—to drag the raging Nathan away from the severely beaten principle. He eventually managed to angrily shrug them off, and realizing they had formed a barrier between him and the head teacher, he snarled and swore several times, then stomped toward the engine. At this point, he cared little what happened to him, and that made Nathan more dangerous than ever.

During the journey back to the station, Nathan was silent the entire way. Captain Mitchell was there to greet them and immediately took Nathan to his office. He was a father himself, so he tried to be sympathetic to Nathan's distress, but it was also his duty to inform him that his assault on the teacher was a serious matter. Mitchell explained that his bosses were already in contact with the principal and trying desperately to persuade him against pressing charges. At present, it looked highly unlikely that he was going to let the matter drop and wanted to punish the animal who'd badly beaten him. The captain immediately suspended Nathan, both for compassionate leave and due to his actions, and told him that Clarissa would drive him home or to the hospital if that was where he wanted to go; he advised against the latter based on Nathan's state of mind. He grabbed his stuff and thanked her for taking him home. He said nothing on the drive to his house and simply stared out the window. Nathan was in a daze, and the reality of that afternoon's events had yet to sink in.

As Nathan sank into a new rage-fueled, alcohol-filled depression, refusing to see his colleagues, Dwayne, or even Lisa, new evidence from the scene of his daughter's death raised serious questions about Nathan's actions. The following day, Peter was reviewing his body cam footage before uploading it to the Fire Service archives, and to his horror noticed something very wrong with what he saw. He immediately alerted Captain Mitchell about what he'd seen and replayed the footage for him. It showed Nathan's fall, which looked innocent enough at first, but when Peter slowed the footage down, there were clear-cut freeze-frame images of Nathan tripping himself up. It also proved that his head never touched the ground, as he had claimed. With his fall looking increasingly fake and question marks about why he had lied about banging his head, Mitchell asked Clarissa to join them in his office. She spent the next hour detailing all her previous concerns about Nathan, and it quickly expanded to include the rest of the station. Once they added some of the other concerning events to the potentially faked fall, such as the "accidental" damage to the football player, the strange incident with the missing equipment that Tom was still adamant wasn't him and the mistakes Doug observed at the large car crash scene, it raised the genuine prospect that Nathan Profit may have deliberately and willfully acted to harm his patients. Everyone now started to second guess all the previously innocuous outcomes. Did he purposely cause extensive pain to the drug dealer? Was it possible that he'd played a part in the death of Officer Russell? Could he have actually assisted the collapsed roof that killed Senator Brooks?

With Nathan becoming ever-more hostile and unhinged at home, he was completely unaware that the fire service had now launched a full-scale official investigation into his conduct and actions. In private and away from the rest of the team, Captain Mitchell, Lieutenant Spencer, and Clarissa also began to contemplate Nathan's private life. If he was capable of all these things at work and truly guilty of harming those he was tasked with helping, what else could he be responsible for?

CHAPTER 13

Nathan thought his life couldn't get any worse. He was absolutely certain during his two years of hell in Afghanistan that it would be impossible for his life to deteriorate any further. The fact he never expected to survive played a large part in that assessment. He would be proved wrong when he finally made it home and found out that his wife had remarried, and he wasn't even allowed to interact with Charlotte as her father. Add the pain of those two events together and surely, he thought, there was nothing more life could do to him that would surpass the pain and heartbreak he'd already endured. It turned out he was wrong. What made it unbearable was the fact that he was responsible for the creation of the abyss-like nightmare that now surrounded him. The grief and self-loathing he felt at being the cause of his daughter's death was all-consuming; his world had literally been obliterated.

Captain Mitchell had initially given Nathan one week of compassionate leave, and then intended to talk to him about his future. His chances of continuing as a first responder were already slim following his savage attack on the principal, but the captain was originally willing to discuss it with Nathan and see if another outcome could be reached. The moment the body cam footage came to light, it eliminated any chance of redemption with the fire service. The assault, the genuine mistakes, the accusations of intentional harm, and his association with a dubiously viewed bar all combined to destroy what little credibility he might have restored following his actions at the school.

Nathan was oblivious to the fast moving investigation that was taking place at the station. Captain Mitchell would have to inform him sooner rather than later, but he still felt a twinge of sympathy for a man who'd just lost his daughter. Throughout his week of compassionate leave, Nathan barely left the house, and even then, it was only to buy more alcohol. He crawled into a bottle to numb his pain and didn't want to come out. In repeated fits of rage and sorrow, he smashed and destroyed almost everything in his house. He burned the photos of his daughter, wrecked his furniture and other things like his television, battered holes in the walls with a baseball bat and even demolished his kitchen. He didn't care, nothing mattered any longer.

Mitchell called, as expected, on the sixth day. Had Nathan bothered to check some of the recordings that were still being made by the bugs in his captain's office, he would have known what was coming. He was aware there would be consequences for his violent outburst at the school, but when he agreed to come to the station the next day, he had no idea the true scale of what was about to be unleashed; during the short call, his boss had simply asked Nathan to attend a meeting the next morning. Following another night with little sleep, he contemplated telling Mitchell to shove his appointment, but he decided to go along anyway; if nothing else, it would present an opportunity for him to tell the world and those in it what he really felt.

Clarissa and Doug were inspecting the truck when Nathan walked into the station. They were utterly shocked at the state of their soon-to-be ex-colleague. He hadn't showered or shaved in days, his short hair was all over the place and it looked, and smelled, like he'd worn the same clothes for a week. The stench of alcohol was almost overwhelming. At least he took a taxi, thought Clarissa. Nathan went straight up to Mitchell's office, where his captain delivered the bombshell news.

"Nathan, I want you to know that the action I take today, I do with a heavy heart. Before we go any further, it gives me no pleasure to officially inform you that, as of this moment, the fire service has placed you on indefinite suspension while internal inspectors carry out an investigation into your conduct," said Mitchell solemnly.

"You know what… yes, I gave that guy a beating. Fuck me, he couldn't even identify that it was my daughter in the water. I am sure any father would have reacted by kicking the daylights out of that useless piece of shit! I hold my hands up; I'm guilty as charged. Like I remotely care about that. Let's cut out all the bullshit; let me know whether I'm facing actual assault charges and then let me get out of here. We all know I can't continue in the job after last week, so let me grab the rest of my stuff and fire me already!" snarled Nathan.

"I'm afraid it's worse than that, Nathan. Peter's body cam footage from the scene of your daughter's accident appears to show you intentionally tripped over and faked banging your head. I can't for the life of me think why, but the only logical answer right now is that you wanted to delay treating the victim for some unfathomable reason," continued Mitchell.

"Now wait a damn minute." interjected Nathan fiercely.

"Nathan, please just be quiet. You are in enough trouble as it is, so for your own sake, I advise you to say nothing more. In addition to your unconscionable delay that killed your own daughter, your colleagues have raised numerous other concerns about things connected to your treatment of patients. We are talking willful negligence, intentional harm, assault, conduct unbecoming, and the very real possibility of manslaughter. The fire service will be terminating your employment in the very near future, there is no doubt about that, but in the meantime, this station will cooperate fully with our own internal inspectors and the police-led criminal investigation that will very likely follow. I can't even begin to comprehend the things you have potentially done. Even if you are found innocent of the charges against you, the assault on the school principal and the question marks around you, proven or not, means you no longer have a place as a first responder. My God, Nathan, what have you done?" concluded a shocked, disgusted, and confused Captain Mitchell.

Nathan stood up, kicked the chair backward and stormed out of the office. He slammed the door so hard that it actually shattered the glass in the top half. Mitchell charged after him, and the two men had an extremely heated argument in the middle of the station. Once they had finished yelling at each other, the captain allowed Nathan to collect his remaining personal belongings and escorted him from the premises. As he walked down the street, Nathan looked back at the station; he wasn't sure if he was sad to lose his job, where he had genuinely helped a lot of people, or happy to be released from its confines.

Later that day, he received several phone calls from both Lisa and Dwayne and refused to answer either of them. A couple of hours later, Lisa showed up at his house and pounded on the front door for nearly thirty minutes. Mitchell had informed her about the investigation into Charlotte's death, including the possibility that Nathan had played a part in it, and she spewed visceral hatred at her ex-husband for killing their daughter. She broke one of the windows by throwing a brick through it and carried on until the police showed up. One of the neighbors had called them and they threatened to arrest her for vandalism, but Nathan told them he didn't want to press charges. It took the two officers nearly ten minutes to talk her into leaving, and they waited until she drove away before they also left. Dwayne turned up unannounced that evening, but even he was turned away by Nathan; he didn't want to see anyone because he had other things on his mind.

One of Nathan's dark web contacts put him in touch with a local gang leader who sold unlicensed weapons. After much deliberation, knowing he now faced the very real possibility that he could eventually be imprisoned for his actions, he changed his original plan to plant bombs at Cross's home. He decided he would confront him, head on and in person, and then either kill him and his family via the intended explosion, or maybe just shoot them all. Nathan had no intention of going to jail because he'd already spent enough of his life as a prisoner; he would rather die first, and that now seemed the only logical outcome to the situation he found himself in. Having purchased a Sturm Ruger P89dc semi-automatic handgun, a regular pump-action shotgun, and a Colt LE6920 semi-automatic rifle, Nathan had everything he needed to deal with Cross.

He spent the next day making a number of explosive devices from the materials that he'd previously purchased. He still hadn't made up his mind how the day would end, but wanted every option available. There was a small thought in his head that he could incinerate the house and simply disappear, but his time with the fire service had taught him that there was usually some form of evidence left over; with only Cross and his family in the ashes, they might work out he didn't perish along with his victims. Nathan loaded up all his weapons and explosives, then drove across town to the street where Cross lived. Wanting to ensure his whole family were there, he placed a webcam in the tree across the road and then parked up in a nearby lot. He watched the house on his cell phone and waited until he knew Cross, his wife, and their three children were all home.

Around 6p.m., Nathan returned to Cross's house, parked his car outside and walked up to the front door. He knocked twice and waited for someone to answer. It was Cross himself who opened the door, and he was somewhat surprised to see Nathan standing there. Without any warning, he immediately brandished the handgun and forced Cross inside. His former senior officer began pleading for the lives of his wife and children straight away, but Nathan didn't want to hear it. At the point of a gun, Nathan forced Cross to tie his wife and children to their chairs at the table. Satisfied they were fully immobilized, he threw two pairs of handcuffs at Cross and made him cuff himself to another chair. Not wanting anyone to cause a problem while he placed the explosives around the house, Nathan injected each of them with a mild anesthetic, and once they were unconscious, he collected the explosive devices and other firearms from the car. Cross came around about an hour later, and by that point Nathan had rigged the doors, windows, and every downstairs room with bombs; he'd even strapped explosives to every member of Cross's family.

Standing imposingly in front of Cross, Nathan told him why he was there. He explained in no uncertain terms that having left him to be tortured and killed in Afghanistan, even when he knew he was still alive and his location, Cross and his family would now pay the price. The colonel managed about four words of begging before Nathan began punching him repeatedly. He beat him so badly that his face began swelling up within minutes. His wife and children screamed and cried, and in the end, Nathan gagged all four of them as he couldn't stand the noise. With the family now quiet, he went back to torturing Cross. Nathan did things to the man that he wouldn't have dreamed of doing prior to his capture in the Middle East. He pulled out half of his fingernails with pliers, slashed his chest with a knife and even drilled through his thighs with an electric tool. Cross was making so much noise with his howls of agony that Nathan eventually had to gag him; after all, there was nothing the man could say to make up for his decision to abandon Nathan in Afghanistan.

Unfortunately for Nathan, his decision to gag Cross while he continued to physically torture him was made too late.

Unknown to him, the neighbors had already heard the repeated screams of pain from Cross and swiftly called the police. His careless and reckless abandonment in the pursuit of revenge had blinded him to even the most obvious of mistakes. From the distance and coming ever closer, the police sirens suddenly dragged Nathan's attention away from the badly injured Colonel to the windows. Within minutes, several police cars had blockaded either end of the street and four others had parked in a semi-circle outside the house. Through a megaphone, they ordered Nathan to lay down his weapons, release his hostages and surrender himself into custody. Using the now untied wife as a shield, he placed his gun to her head and walked to the window. After she had opened it, he yelled back that he had the whole family hostage and wouldn't surrender until he'd finished what he'd started. When asked what he meant by that, he merely responded by telling the senior police officer that they'd find out soon enough.

Out of the corner of his eye, he spotted the arrival of a S.W.A.T. van. Although angry with himself for being so foolhardy that he'd inadvertently attracted the attention of the neighbors, he'd always known this was one possible outcome. Moving back slightly from the window, he yelled at the police that he had booby-trapped all the entrances, and if the S.W.A.T. team stormed the house, everyone would be killed. To make sure they understood that he wasn't bluffing, he identified himself, so they knew he was an ex-marine. To buy time, Nathan hinted that he might be willing to let the children go if the police kept their distance. With Cross's wife tied up again, Nathan went back to work, inflicting pain and brutal punishment on the colonel.

About an hour after the police arrived, there was a shout over the megaphone that they had someone who wanted to speak to Nathan. He peered out of the window and saw Lisa standing near one of the cars. There was a part of him that would have loved to just open fire with the Colt rifle and kill her right where she stood, but he knew that would bring everything to a swift, bloody end, and he wasn't finished yet. She pleaded with him to turn himself in to the police, to let Cross and his family go free, but he knew her well enough to realize that the tone in her voice meant she didn't really mean what she was saying. To get rid of her, and to avoid the possibility of a rash, impulsive action, Nathan shouted out that if they didn't take her away, he'd shoot her in the next ninety seconds. Not taking any chances, she was immediately ushered away. As she got into a car to go back home, she suggested they might want to reach out to Dwayne and see if his best friend could talk Nathan down.

When he arrived, he volunteered to approach the house in full view of Nathan with his hands held aloft. At first, he made the same threat to Dwayne as he had to Lisa, but after literally begging his friend to let him help, Nathan allowed Dwayne into the house. As he stood just inside the closed front door, he could see the family all tied up in the dining room. Being a marine himself, he also observed all the explosives attached to them, and around the doors and windows. He tried to talk to Nathan, to make him see reason, and to understand that killing Cross and his family wouldn't bring Charlotte back. He quickly realized that Nathan was well aware of that, and that his present course of action was nothing more than pure revenge. Dwayne couldn't believe that Nathan was pointing a gun at him, and in his present state of mind, he had no idea if he would actually shoot him. Shocked by the savagery of Cross's wounds, Dwayne attempted to appeal to whatever part might still exist of the old Nathan Profit that he knew and loved.

Dwayne was wasting his time because Nathan was now too far gone. The sight of Lisa and now his best friend had reminded him of all the things he'd lost, and the man responsible was at his mercy. He poured out all his anger and hate about what Cross had done, for being the man who had ultimately denied permission for a rescue attempt. Refusing to give in, his best friend pleaded with him, over and over, to give himself up and seek the help he so clearly needed. He got Nathan to look over at Cross's terrified children, trying desperately to reach some form of empathy that might still be buried deep within the man opposite him. For just a few seconds, he saw what looked like a moment of hesitation in his friend's eyes. Dwayne grabbed it with both hands, and implored Nathan to let the wife and children go.

He played a risky strategy and told Nathan he wouldn't leave the house unless it was with Cross's family. Nathan didn't want to kill Dwayne; he bore no responsibility in what happened, and as much as he wanted equal retribution and to take Cross's family with him, he eventually relented to avoid killing his best friend. Nathan agreed he would let Cross's wife and children leave the house with Dwayne, but not Cross himself. He gave Dwayne permission, still with a gun pointed at him, to free the rest of the family. Worried his clearly deranged friend might change his mind, Dwayne quickly untied everyone. He ushered them to the door and looked over at Nathan for a final confirmation he was going to allow them to leave; he nodded his approval. Dwayne stood in the open door, visibly upset, and begged him one last time to give himself up.

"Thank you for always being there, my friend. My journey is over, and so is the life of that bastard in there who cost me everything with his inaction. Goodbye, Dwayne… it has been an honor."

Nathan closed the door with Dwayne still standing there and walked into the room with Cross. He sat down on a chair and wept, and at that point decided upon his final course of action. Nathan stood up and walked over to Cross with a look of remorse on his face. He explained he couldn't kill his family and that he just wanted the world to know what happened. The vengeful marine gave him hope that he would tell his story and release Cross to face the music. Standing near the window, Nathan poured out his heart to everyone who was listening, knowing full well that the multitude of journalists and reporters were within earshot. He told them everything, then explained he would let everyone else be the judge. He walked over to Cross and acted like he was about to let him go, and when he saw the relief in Cross's eyes that he thought he was going to be set free, he knew he'd achieved what he wanted.

"Sorry, Colonel," he said with derision and malice. "I just changed my mind. You cost me my wife, my daughter... my life... and now I take yours!"

With a vicious, evil smile, he reached into his pocket and pulled out a detonator.

"I'll see you in hell..."

The house suddenly exploded in a giant fireball... and Nathan Profit had extracted his final revenge. There is an old saying that declares those who seek revenge should dig two graves; never was an old adage so appropriate. Dwayne sat on the other side of the road and could do nothing more than watch the first responders put out the intense blaze caused by the blast. He was heartbroken that he had failed to save his friend, but had to accept he'd done all he could.

Days later, as the investigation continued, a local church held a memorial service for Nathan; only Dwayne, Clarissa, and Captain Mitchell attended. Lisa told everyone she was glad he was rotting in hell. By comparison, Colonel Cross had a huge funeral that was attended by everyone, including Dwayne, Lisa, members of Nathan's station, countless dignitaries, and even the media.

A few weeks after the blast, questions started to arise. They had found numerous remains of Colonel Cross, which had since been buried, but as far as Nathan was concerned, they only found an ear—that was a confirmed match via DNA—his watch and his dog tags. As Washington P.D. detectives, fire service inspectors and forensic specialists investigated the burnt out remains of the house, the consensus grew that Nathan may not have died in the blast. Several people suggested he'd done a shitty job with laying out his explosive devices and that their pattern appeared to kill in certain directions, but only maim in others. Even Dwayne confirmed it was unlikely Nathan had made a mistake like that. It raised the very real possibility that Nathan had walked away from the fire.

When it was announced some weeks later that the authorities believed he was probably still alive... the hunt for Nathan Profit had begun...

www.ingramcontent.com/pod-product-compliance
Lightning Source LLC
Chambersburg PA
CBHW061301120726
48001CB00001B/419